"Do you think I'm gay?" she asked casually.

I gazed up at her, suddenly considering that I might have moved too hastily with Rachel. I didn't know if I should dignify the question with an answer so I remained silent.

She was serious. "How do I know?"

"You just know, that's all. It's like being French. Either you are, or you're not."

Rachel dove on top of me. "Put your arms around me and tell me you love me."

I stretched my arms wide and let them fall tightly around her. "I love you."

"You do?" she asked playfully.

"You're a nut."

She whispered in my ear. "And you are a goddess." An electric current traveled from my inner ear through the length of my body, setting off a burning charge between my thighs.

Clockwise—The stars and filmmakers of "BAR GIRLS." NANCY ALLISON WOLFE, CAMILA GRIGGS, LAURAN HOFFMAN (writer/producer), LISA PARKER, JUSTINE SLATER, MARITA GIOVANNI (director/producer), LIZA D'AGOSTINO.

Photo credit: Fred Valentine

by
Lauran Hoffman

THE NAIAD PRESS, INC.
1996

Printed in the United States of America on acid-free paper
First Edition

Editor: Lisa Epson
Cover designer: Bonnie Liss (Phoenix Graphics)
Typesetter: Sandi Stancil

Library of Congress Cataloging-in-Publication Data

Hoffman, Lauran, 1963 –
Bar girls / by Lauran Hoffman.
p. cm.
ISBN 1-56280-115-5
1. Lesbians—California—Los Angeles—Fiction. 2. Gay bars—California—Los Angeles—Fiction. 3. Los Angeles (Calif.)—Fiction. I. Title.
PS3558.03455B37 1995
813′.54—dc20 95-25553
CIP

Dedicated to
Liza, Laurie, and Gabrielle
and
Big Love
to
My family and all our exes

Special Acknowledgments

Big Doug Lindeman, Maxwell Pennock Jr., Pleasant Gehman, Brandon Behrstock, Leeanne Stables, Anne Mette Johnsen, Steven C. Schechter, Wendy (you'll always be Hoffman to me) Stinchfield, Greg Hoffman, Marita Giovanni, Michael and Peri Ferris, Nicole Ferris, Anke Thommen, Jay Albala, Celia Albala, P. J. Lindeman, the Ringling Sisters, Club 22, Nancy Kesterson, Robert Pennington, Liza (Tiny Mighty) D'Agostino, Justine (Tenacious) Slater, Chas (Buddy) Bono, Betsy (the Goddess) Burke, Nancy Allison Wolfe, Camila Griggs, Lauren (Lisa) Parker, Michael Harris, Pam Raines, Paula Sorge, Cece Tsou, Caitlin Stansbury, Patti Sheehan, Lee Everett, T. J. (Too Hot to Fish) McCall, Trista Delamere, Laurie Jones, Kristin (wish I could have been there) Klier, Monica Watford, Victoria Vaughn, Lauren (No Details) Hanson, Randy (Soulmate) Kirby, Jeanie Mikkelsen, Christie Peck, WilmaPEZ, Wendy Slutsky, Lynn Markert, Greg Morris, Jennifer Fisher, E. Blair McKinney, Wisconsin Sturm, Ellen Whelpton, Glen Russell, Laura Lamastro, Jennifer Rhodes, Maria Lynn, Kathy Wolfe, Liz Salaway, Judy Torres, Mark Shoenberg, Patricia Taudien, the Heart-Breaking Grant sisters, Patrick Hutchinson, Dave Catchings, Michael Cox, The Palms, Girl Bar, Barbara Grier, Orion Classics, Sara Rose, Bob Berney, Scott Mandell, Jay Peckos, Marina Bailey, Herb Dorfman, Jonna Winnicki, Jim Jensen, Pacific Shore Media, Ray Hoboush, Tom Conroy, Gary Horowitz, Sheila Horowitz, Julie Horowitz, Eva Eklund, Tracy Johnson, Robin Haar, Brita M. Engseth, Andrea Isco, Female FYI, Heidi Shink, Donna Isman, Amy Ruskin, Red, Brian, and Paul.

About the Author

Lauran Lee Hoffman was born in Chicago, Illinois, in 1963, although she only lived there a year and consequently didn't get out much. In 1964 her family set forth for Los Angeles where they pursued a lifestyle of extreme hippy decadence. Lauran grew up surrounded by friends that could usually be found camped out in a tent in the backyard. They had names like D'Artagnan and Snake. She and her siblings were always told to "make love, not war" — until they got old enough to make love, and then the slogans began to change.

At age twelve, her mother got the Jed Clampett syndrome mixed up and loaded up the truck to move to Atascadero — Hicksville, that is.

Lauran found the transition from city rat to country mouse extremely difficult. In the city she had lots of juvenile delinquent friends; she had the RTD system wired so she was completely mobile; and she always knew where the best sales were. In the country all the kids just sat around chewing tobacco and waiting for a gopher to peep its innocent head out of a hole so they could blow it off with their pa's .22. Once they got their driver's license they would see how fast they could hit an oak tree without totaling their Ford truck.

Eventually Lauran managed to graduate with the school's highest GPA, 1.65, and then went on to achieve extended academic probation at a local junior college (not quite a college, but close). After two years of heavy bribery and debauchery, she managed to get her associate of arts degree and went to a university where she opted for a dual major — fruit science and animal husbandry. She moved back to Los Angeles and earned a bachelor's degree in a lucrative field in which she had absolutely no interest. Determined to make poetry hip again, she avidly pursued a career as a poet, traveling from town to town spewing forth wise, pithy profundities about love and pain and the whole damn thing.

On June 10, 1993, she mounted her first full-length play, *Bar Girls,* at The Gene Dynarski Theater in Hollywood, California. One year later, in September 1994, she had finished her first full-length feature film. *Bar Girls,* the film, was written and produced by Hoffman and distributed nationally by Orion Classics in 1995. Her newest film project, *Soul Mates,* is now in development.

Due to some glitch in the universe's programming, she is currently single. She lives in the Hollywood Hills with her three golden retrievers.

1

I want to be in love and have the person I love, love me more. Although if she loved me more, I'd love her less, which eventually would be not at all. No, I want to be in love equally. That would be perfect — at least for a while. Until we get too close to each other. Then issues arise and she decides she needs space. And she goes out in search of space but discovers a great void in all that space. So she finds someone to fill that void, and it is never me. She doesn't even look like me.

When two people break up they each become

exactly what the other person always wanted them to be, but they are no longer interested in each other. Some people think I'm bitter, and I am, but I'm always willing to be hurt again.

I was getting dressed to go out to the bar for a date with Annie, the athlete. Annie, whose skin smelled like bananas because she ate at least five whole Chiquitas a day. I was infatuated with Annie. Well, that's the word I use to save face after someone I'm in love with leaves me. "Annie? Come on, I didn't love her. I was infatuated."

The "Tonight, Tonight" song from *West Side Story* was playing on a loop tape in my head. This was nothing new. The song had plagued me since I was eight. I threw on my usual outfit: black. Black everything — pants, shirt, black leather jacket, black boots. Black makes me look thinner. I can hear my mother in my head, "You have to wear some color, all black is not good." Why it's not good, she never clarified. All right already, must I carry an internalized mother and therapist in my head? So I changed. In fact, not only did I try on every outfit I have, I seriously considered rifling through my neighbors' closets. I threw every discarded piece of clothing on my bed and ended up wearing the black. Black is best. I decided to wear the red ring I have for color.

Once I was dressed I had to get out of the house immediately. There is something scary about walking around your house all alone and dressed up for an evening out. It's too easy to kill yourself. All the elements are there.

I grabbed my car keys, jumped into my car, and backed down the driveway. My car reaffirms the fact that some material things can actually bring me happiness. It's a customized 300 ZX chop-top convertible with turbo charge and nitrous oxide injection, which I'll never use. Someone once told me never to drive faster than my angels can fly. So what about plane travel?

Moments later I was at Club 22, the perfect bar for me. It had such a small-town quality it should have had a population sign. I'd walk in and every girl in the place would look up as if to say, Who's here? The decor was hard to describe since there wasn't much light to see it with. There was a nicely lit jukebox by the front door and two pool tables, which were smaller than regulation but big enough to lay a stick on, were off to the side. I walked straight (forward, never straight) to the bar. I had an adrenaline rush coursing through me that only a double Stoli with a splash of cran would cure, or so I thought at the time. Celia was behind the bar, which meant every third drink would be on the house. There were a few girls seated strategically in front of the bar, but even on a Thursday it was looking pretty dead.

Celia had owned Club 22 since the first lesbian discovered she was one. Of course, Celia claimed her as a girlfriend. Celia was attractive despite her wisdom. She had red hair that screamed cellophane and a nice lean body due to years of aerobics instruction. I once had an aerobics instructor who was also my gynecologist, and I thought that that was intrusive. Celia and I were close friends, but we didn't see each other outside of the bar. We hardly even saw each other inside, the bar was so damned dark.

I stood at the bar. I never sit at bars. It's a bad position to be in if you want to maintain any sense of power. Celia saw me immediately and scooted on over.

"Hey, Loretta, what's cookin', sugar?"

"I've got a date with Psycho Jock."

"Did you bring bananas for her muscle cramps?"

"No, but I brought a hacksaw so she could cut that cord to her ex."

Celia leaned over the bar and planted a kiss on me that would never come off. Celia could have been the mother I never had, if I'd never had a mother. Since I did, she was almost too much.

She got me my usual drink, and I waited for Annie BananaPores. I waited way past *Cosmopolitan*'s suggested time limit for a late date. I looked at the front door and imagined Annie walking in toward me. She was tall, which was usually desirable, but she was taller than me, which wasn't. She walked gracefully and fluidly, as if she were filled with hydrogen and could float away if I didn't step on her feet to keep her grounded. She always wore strategically ripped blue jeans that sexily showed the quadricep muscles on her long legs. I wondered if other girls had heart palpitations when they saw her or if it was just me. The sandy blond hair that dove down her shoulders had to have been matched with her pale complexion by a professional colorist. Annie had the deepest blue eyes, like the waters off the continental shelf where the sharks dwell. Sometimes I swore I could see sharks swimming around her pupils.

She never showed up. I had wasted my black outfit. I said good-bye to C, walked outside the club, and stood on the sidewalk for a second to give Annie one more chance. Annie must've gotten tied up. She must have had a good reason, I told myself as my pal Tracy walked up to the club.

Tracy was from South Carolina, but I didn't hold that against her. She was a big, bleached blond, butchie type who could scare a poolball into its pocket with a single stare. This particular night she was wearing her Harley Davidson shirt tucked smartly into her big work slacks. Her wallet and keys were snug in her back pocket and attached to her pants with a bulky Diesel chain. Her looks were misleading though, because she was gentle and as mild mannered as a magnolia tree.

Tracy nearly snapped my spine with a hug. I told her how long I'd been waiting for Annie.

"Come on in with me. We'll play some pool," Tracy said, as she gave my arm a tug.

"Nah, I think I'm gonna split. Getting stood up really quells my ambition." I looked at my car, wishing it were Annie.

Tracy took out a pack of American Spirit Tobacco and began to roll herself a cigarette as she spoke. "I don't know why I come here night after night, to see the same old boring faces, looking as disappointed with me as I am with them."

"I know what you mean. I'm gonna hit it."

I was edging toward my car when I felt something special approaching. I slowly turned my head to the right. Walking up the street toward us was a woman I had never seen before. I looked at her feet and instantly felt like I was in a western. She wore gray ringtail lizard cowboy boots, black leggings, a tan silk shirt, and a tight blue riding jacket. Her hair was so long and curly that it bounced against her shoulders with each step she took. Time stalled. It was as if I was seeing her in slow motion. I followed her movement with my whole body. I turned a full one-eighty and watched her as she confidently walked right between us and into the club.

I was still staring at the front door as it swung shut. "Maybe I'll hang," I said to Tracy.

"Hell, after that stare I wouldn't be surprised if you spent the night." Tracy gave me a little pat to knock me from my trance. She then swung around me and pushed open the door as I walked back into the club.

We stood at the entrance looking for this new woman. Tracy spotted her first and gave me a nudge. She was over by the pool tables talking to a few girls and shaking hands. The two girls she was with were a couple. Of what I couldn't say. I had to meet this woman and I had to move fast. Tracy and I sidled up to the bar.

"Hey C, how ya doin'?" Tracy took a long drag off her cigarette and blew the smoke out sideways.

Celia wiped her hands on her bar rag. "Well, my shoes are too tight and my bar is dyin', but besides that . . ." She began to fix Tracy a soda water with a splash of cranberry. Tracy and Celia had been friends longer than either of them cared to remember. They shared a ritual between them. Celia would slide Tracy's drink down the bar right before Tracy asked for it. This evening their timing was perfect, which wasn't always the case. Celia slid the glass smooth and quick, and Tracy snatched it up like it had been in front of her all along.

Tracy took a sip. "You know C, you oughta try havin' some theme nights. It did real good business for bars back home. Everybody'd dress up like Bonanza characters and stuff."

Celia lifted an eyebrow, both acknowledging and dismissing this idea instantly. She turned to me without a word to Trace. "Lo, what can I get ya?"

"You see that beautiful woman over there?" I lamely pointed in the new girl's direction.

Celia squinted myopically across the room. "Loretta, with these eyes I can't see anything, but assuming there is a girl, and you say she's beautiful, what do you want me to do about it?"

"I would like to buy her a drink. Any drink she wants." My eyes remained fixed on this gorgeous new girl.

"Well, that's big of you," Celia joked.

As she turned to leave, I grabbed her arm. "Wait, there is a catch. You can't tell her who is sending her the drink, okay?"

"Whatever turns you on." Celia gave the bar a good wipe and walked to the pool tables to see the new gal.

Tracy and I headed for a table by the dance floor in an attempt to remain invisible. I tried not to watch Celia's progress. Celia got the order and sauntered back to the bar and began to fix drinks.

The starting lineup bartender, Kimba, a winning blond combo of boyish good looks, charisma, and a smile hot enough to melt metal, flirted with four girls who were tipping themselves bankrupt. Celia was constantly annoyed by Kimba's popularity with the chicks. Let's face it, we were all annoyed with Kimba. Who needed competition from a bartender?

Celia walked up behind Kimba. "You wanna clean those glasses?" Celia chided. Celia was always eager to undermine Kimba's posturings.

Kimba jumped slightly, then cringed with embarrassment.

"Not a problem," Kimba responded, recovering her composure so quickly that all the girls saw was a perky grin.

I think that Tracy was telling me about the carburetor she was rebuilding on her truck, but all I heard were the new girl's boots clicking on the floor as she approached the bar to talk to Celia.

They seemed to be laughing a little too much. I wondered what Celia was telling her. I thought to myself, What am I getting so bent for? I have a girlfriend, kind of. I'm a happening chick. I'm not needy. I'd decided to take a quick risk and if it didn't pay off, so what.

I interrupted Tracy's truck tales. "If I can't get that girl in my car in ten minutes, I'm leaving."

Tracy smiled at me. "Well, you have to draw the line somewhere, I guess . . ."

"Tracy, you can have anyone you want in this life if you possess three simple qualities: patience, charisma, and patience."

"Well then, all you lack is charisma." Tracy kicked one foot up on a chair and savored her own wit.

"Maybe we'll fall madly in love, and I could ditch the psycho who stood me up tonight."

"I've always wondered why you get together with women who treat you like dirt," Tracy said as she twisted up another smoke.

"I'm used to being treated like dirt. When people

treat me well, I get suspicious. It makes me think they want something from me."

Tracy's eyebrows fused together. "Yeah, like your friendship."

"No, that would be too easy. They treat me well in preparation to fuck me over. I trust people who fuck me over right away; it's more honest."

Celia squeezed past Kimba and her groupies, bent over the table, and spoke to us softly. "She keeps asking me who sent the drink. Can I tell her or what?"

I stayed back against my seat so as not to blow my cover. "Okay. Tell her I sent the drink, but tell her I told you not to tell her and you decided to tell her on your own."

"You're strange," said Celia, shooting me her number four glance of condescension and walking slowly back to the bar.

Tracy slurped up the rest of her soda and smacked her glass on the table. "What's the point?"

"This way she'll think I'm shy, which is a good edge. Then she can approach me if she's interested. If not, I don't have to be embarrassed, 'cause she'll think that I had no intention of making contact anyway." I slapped my hands together, proud of the whole scenario.

"That's pretty slick."

We both looked toward the new gal just as she headed our way. "Oh shit, here she comes."

Tracy and I jumped up as this beautiful babe flashed a smile that could excite Anita Bryant. I extended my hand awkwardly for a shake. "Hi, I'm Loretta. How ya doin'?"

"I'm great," she beamed. "Thanks for the drink."

"Oh. She told you. She wasn't supposed to," I said loud enough for Celia to hear.

We all turned and looked at Celia standing behind the bar kneading her rag, looking sheepish. Finally got one over on Celia. I looked at Tracy, who couldn't take a hint if it were her birthday present.

"Uh, this is my friend Tracy."

Tracy looked back and forth at each of us, and started to get the picture. "Well, I'm gonna go mingle." We let her go, but our eyes remained on each other.

"A Southern 'mingler'." I sometimes speak when silence is preferable.

"I'm Rachel."

She warmed more than my heart with her magnificent smile.

"Are you from New York, Rachel?"

"How could you tell?"

"You have that I'm-never-gonna-get-mugged-again ambience."

"Oh, you could tell by my accent," she laughed.

"Yeah." We stood idly for an awkward moment. "Do you play pool?"

"Yeah, I can knock 'em around. Do you play?"

"I'm almost unbeatable," I lied. "I've been known to get balls in on tables I wasn't even playing on at the time."

We headed over to the pool tables and picked out sticks. I prefer a twenty-one. She went for a twenty. I wondered if she noticed I was studying every inch of her. She had perfect olive skin, sparkling brown eyes, winged eyebrows, and full, succulent lips like an extra erogenous zone. Her accent said Bronx. She must have been Italian or Puerto Rican. I guessed both.

"You have a very New York sense of humor. Has anyone ever told you that?" she said, seemingly oblivious to my scrutiny.

"Only people from New York. People from Idaho tell me I have a very Idaho sense of humor. I'm kind of a humor chameleon."

I noticed Tracy seated on the pool table behind Rachel's back. A big grin was thrown at me, just in case I wasn't fully aware that she'd been spying. She pointed to her wristwatch and made a circular clockwise motion with her index finger, indicating that the minutes were ticking away. I remembered my self-imposed time limit and grabbed Rachel's arm.

"I want you to go with me for a ride in my car."

"Why would I want to do that?" she flirted.

"Because you're intrigued by me," I blurted out, surprised when it sounded okay.

"Oh yeah, why should I trust you?" She edged back.

"You should never trust anyone who tries too hard to make you trust 'em."

"Pretty sure of yourself, aren't you?" She walked around me sizing me up for the kill.

"I try not to analyze things too much."

Rachel looked through my soul right to my shoes. "I think you analyze yourself until you've forgotten what you were analyzing."

"Let's try not to get too analytical on our first meeting, or we may cancel ourselves out before we ever get to argue over who gets the furniture when we break up."

"Okay," she said, making my knees suddenly weaken, "let's go."

"Really?" I asked, genuinely surprised.

"Cold feet?"

"Warm heart. Let's try to keep it that way,"

"Should we divide up that furniture now?" she joked as we put our pool cues back on the rack and headed for the door.

"I get the dining room set, you can have the waterbed."

Rachel walked out. I lagged behind. Tracy gave me our secret hang-loose gesture; I returned the favor and turned to leave.

Tracy took a long drag off her smoke and surveyed the girls in the pool room. "Rack 'em up," she announced, "I feel hot tonight!"

2

Rachel and I walked to my car. I opened the passenger door for her, which is a little trick I use sparingly, and only until dating turns to something else. She unlocked my door before I got around to it — always a good sign. I started up the engine and asked her to excuse me while I reached between her legs. She blushed slightly and obliged me. I slowly reached beneath her seat and removed my pull-out stereo. I slid it in its holster, pulled out my case of lesbian friendly CDs, and popped in some

Annie Lennox. We raced out of the parking spot, and I took her through the gears.

The music was blasting too loudly for us to talk to each other. We just looked ahead shyly, and every so often we'd catch each other staring at the other. We'd laugh and look back at the road. I drove her up to Mulholland and around the notorious turns which were bordered by hills and cliffs. It was a warm and beautifully clear summer night. The lights across the city flickered secret, Morse code messages as we took in each moment of the evening. I drove down Laurel Canyon to Santa Monica Boulevard. I wanted to show her off to the gay and lesbian section of town and vice versa. We cruised by The Palms, Micky's, Rage, and I swung my little tour past the Girl Bar to end it off with a bang.

I asked Rachel if she wanted to go back to her car or if she wanted to come home with me and look at my phone doodles. It wasn't that I wanted to have sex with Rachel, I just wanted to get to know her better very quickly.

I pulled into my driveway and left the car engine running. I don't know what possessed me. Maybe it was the hard driving beat of the Diva CD, maybe it was the moonlight. Or maybe it was because I felt so comfortable with Rachel. Whatever it was, I jumped out of the car and started doing this crazy little headlight dance in front of the car. I got into the music and let my body get loose and wild. I spun around, danced, and even started getting kind of risque, bumping and grinding like a stripper. Rachel seemed pleased with my act and got up on the edge of her seat to see me better. I lustily climbed onto the hood of my car and crawled slowly up to the windshield. I could feel the warmth of the engine and its vibration against my whole body. I reached my hands up to the top of the windshield and slid myself all the way up until I was face to face with Rachel. She was laughing and I started to laugh too. I felt so close to her I could have kissed her right then, but we both became shy and I slipped back beneath the window's protective shield. I swung my legs around and jumped off the car. She applauded. I turned off the engine and said, "Well, this is my house," and we both started laughing at the strange way I had introduced my house.

Even though I had my own place, I still felt like someone else owned it and I was just taking care of it until they came home. I tried not to put any holes in the walls or make too much noise at night. I wondered if I'd ever feel like an adult, although I never really felt like a kid either. I was a very tame child. I was average. In fact, they designed the bell curve around me. I was top of the bell. While all my friends were cutting classes and spinning three-sixties in their cars in the school parking lot, I was in class reading Flaubert's *Madame Bovary* and thinking what a slut she was. But I wanted to be a rebel; I wanted to be reckless; I wanted to lose my virginity to a carny while the circus was in town. Instead, I would sit at home watching "Laverne and Shirley" in my footsie pajamas. I was never wild. Even in preschool, I was afraid to nap.

We walked up to the front door and I fumbled with my keys, finally managing to unlock my door in spite of its secret agenda to expand and contract at the most inopportune times. I let her walk first into my den of iniquity. Rachel took in the space by examining every inch of the living and dining rooms from a few key positions.

My house is furnished with an eclectic mixture of art pieces and furniture. A blue-and-red colored mosaic-tiled, five-foot coffee shrine stood in the dining room. Rachel noticed it instantly. "Like coffee, do ya?" she said sarcastically, and then she nearly walked into my female manikin leg that hung from the ceiling sporting a blue eight-holed Dr. Martens laced to her foot.

Posters of Billie Holiday, Rita Hayworth, and Lotte Lenya adorned the living room walls. "Lotte Lenya. I love her music," Rachel said, transfixed by her picture. My TV console was a large and angular plastic construction, à la a *Jetson's* accessory. I'd always felt that it accented the living room and embellished the process of TV viewing with a certain *je ne sais quoi.* To complete the arrangement, I had positioned a ceramic pot filled with fresh flowers atop the console.

I keyed up some funky dance music, and we began to dance around the room in a parody of coolness as we tried to one-up each other in weirdness. You can always tell if someone is good at something by their ability to satirize the medium.

Rachel was wild on the floor. She'd jump from hip-hop to modern to some country two-step, then she'd pretend not to know where the beat was and she'd snap her fingers to find it, jumping back into the music like a pro. I fell on the couch laughing uncontrollably. She danced in front of me, making crazy round-the-mountain gestures with her arms and laughing at the same time. Suddenly she stopped dancing and looked at me sprawled out on the couch.

My legs were casually spread apart and I could see Rachel had noticed and had become uncomfortable. It was a clear case of sexuality rearing its lovely head and ruining our spontaneity. It had reminded her that we were virtually strangers.

A look of nervousness crossed her face. "Well, maybe I should go . . ."

I sat up and pulled myself together. "Really, why? I mean . . . you are free to go. You're not my prisoner or anything . . . yet."

Rachel loosened up with this remark and sat down next to me on the couch. "Don't scare me."

"I'm having fun. Why don't you stay a little while?"

She looked around the house. "I don't know. It doesn't look like you have much furniture to divide."

"No, but I have lots of stuff."

"Yeah, you sure do. And what do you do to attain all this stuff?"

"I have a job," I said as I tried to remember what I did for a living.

"No shit?" She smirked.

"Yeah. I write for a cartoon series on cable."

"Oh, I love cartoons. What's it called?"

"You've never heard of it," I downplayed.

"I might have," she persisted. "What's it called?"

" 'Heavy Myrtle'. She's this zaftig couple's counseling superhero. Due to her special powers, she can sense when a couple is having relationship problems and she swoops into their lives to give them free counseling."

Rachel hesitated. "No, I never heard of it. Sounds great though."

"Hey, wanna see my bedroom?"

Rachel laughed. "Nice segue."

"Did ya like that?" I smiled.

"Yeah." She sat next to me on the arm of the sofa.

"So . . . do you wanna see my bedroom?"

"Pretty eager."

"Rachel, if I wanted to seduce you I would have kissed you by now. Or at least I'd have looked deeply into your eyes." I looked deeply into her eyes. "I like to lie on my bed with my friends; it's more intimate. You're really safe, you know, 'cause I'm actually seeing someone right now."

She leaned back confidently. "That's cool, 'cause I'm married . . ."

"No shit?"

". . . to a man." Rachel sprang this news casually. She got up and walked across the living room and started browsing through my CD collection.

"That's a bummer," I said.

"What do you care? You're in love with someone anyway." She pulled out my CD of Barbra Streisand's *Christmas Album*. Maybe that was what had caused the perplexed look on her face.

"Yeah, . . . well, I am . . . actually, so is she, but I think it's with somebody else. Or herself. I'm not quite sure."

"Well, I'm actually not very married right now. But I am seeing a woman I like way too much."

"What's too much?" I attempted to swallow this disappointing information. I'm a Scorpio. It is said that Scorpios will travel through lifetimes to avenge a simple parking ticket. It's nothing for me to get jealous over people who don't even exist.

"At all." She returned the Streisand CD. "Let's see your bedroom." Slowly she slinked toward me and offered her hand. I hesitated for a moment while she gave me a come-hither motion with her fingers. I rose, took her hand, and led her down the narrow hallway into the bedroom.

I had forgotten about all the clothes I had piled on my bed hours earlier while trying to find the perfect ensemble. "Sorry it's such a mess," I said as I pushed all the clothes off of the bed and onto the floor. Oh great, now she probably thought I was a slob and a slut.

"This is nothin'. At least we can walk through it," she said, softening the situation.

I leapt backward onto my king-sized waterbed like I'd been thrown by an unseen force. I kicked off my shoes. At least the bed beneath the closet's contents had been neatly made and covered with a huge white down comforter. Oversize, fluffy down pillows were piled against the ornate, carved wood headboard. I looked up to find Rachel studying my actions. "Have a seat."

Rachel slid off her boots and sank amidst the sea of down. She managed to find a sock I had missed, and she started twirling it around to tease me. We smiled at each other as some magical, magnetic force wrapped us in twine and began tightening the pull between us. We simultaneously fell toward each other, mouths poised for imminent kisses. Another unexpected wave of shyness swept over me, and I stopped just short of her lips. I turned my head away from her, not knowing what to make of my own behavior.

My reaction caught her by surprise. She began swinging the sock again. "So, you don't wanna do the grown up — whatcha got in mind?"

"Grown up?" I knew the phrase, but I wanted to mask my surprise at her assumption that I wanted to have sex. "No, let's — let's just visit."

"Parents visit," she corrected me. "Let's hang out."

"Yeah, so, you're married?" I was pulling at my shirt to make sure it was covering my stomach. Everyone has their own insecurities, and one of mine is my stomach. How do people have flat stomachs when they're seated?

"Oh. You did mean visit," She joked.

"Okay, okay, too personal." I tried to quell my feelings of awkwardness.

Rachel found a solution. "Tell you what let's do." She shifted her body toward me excitedly and finally dropped the sock. "You tell me about your girlfriends, and I'll tell you about mine. You start."

"Oh, well," I laughed, trying to think. "I'd have to start with my current nightmare: Annie, the psycho athlete from Bakersfield. You know, I wasn't even that crazy about her when I met her three months ago. The first night we went out, we went to Malibu."

I fluffed up the pillows behind me to get comfortable. I lay down and took myself back to that night out on the beach.

The full moon was hanging over the ocean like a big orange sucker. Annie was wearing white cut-offs and a bare midriff shirt. Her body sported a lovely brown tan she had acquired from sunbathing in the nude. Annie picked up a rock and threw it way out into the water. She then began to stretch her long body, her thoughts never far from her physical plane.

"One day I'm gonna swim in a triathlon competition," she insisted.

"One day, I'm gonna learn to swim," I responded. I managed to avoid the wave making a beeline for my Frye boots by taking a quick jog backward.

She grabbed me, put her arms around me, and hugged me tightly. "You are so fun and wonderful, do you know that?"

I remained silent, soaking up the compliment. She took a deep breath of ocean air and exhaled loudly. The air that night was calm and slightly chilly. We looked out across the ocean. A strange thought occurred to me.

"Look at those waves," I said, gazing hypnotically off to the horizon. "It looks like they don't have a care in the world. Do you think that some waves out in the middle of the ocean wait all of eternity to get one chance to touch the shore? I think those are a wave's aspirations."

Annie looked at me intensely. "I could seriously fall in love with you."

I didn't know how to respond to her, and luckily I didn't have to. She kept right on talking. "Loretta, I have to tell you . . . I'm living with a woman I'm in love with. I should have told you last night, but . . . I was having such a blast . . . are you mad at me?" she said, swaying her body back and forth.

"No, unfortunately, I'm even more interested." Overcome with the desire I experience every time I find a woman who is unavailable, I lunged forward and kissed Annie vigorously.

It wasn't long before we were entwined like a double helix, all wrapped up around each other without even connecting.

Annie pulled back suddenly. "Let's make love right here on the beach! Under the stars and the moon . . ."

"And that Chevy up there with its lights on — they've been watching us ever since you lobbed that boulder into the water."

"They won't see us . . ." She yanked me down on my knees into the cold moist sand.

"I can't." I extended my hands and began to lightly massage the soft skin of her muscular shoulders. It almost made me reconsider.

She began rubbing me all over my arms and back. "Why not?" she said as she snuck a kiss onto my neck.

I was getting excited but I tried to hold my ground. "It just takes me a while to warm up to someone sexually, you know."

She shook her head as though she understood. "I'm weird," I admitted. A prude was more like it.

"You're not weird. What is it? Is it me?" she asked sweetly.

I held her hands admiring her long fingers. "No, it's not you, you're great. I just have this thing . . . you know, I have to be in love to do it." She brought my hands to her mouth and kissed both making sure neither would be jealous.

"I can understand that. I'll wait."

"What about your girlfriend?"

"We don't make love," she said as she moved out from my embrace.

I was shocked. "Ever?"

"She's straight," she replied, averting her eyes from mine.

I moved closer to see her expression. She seemed embarrassed by her admission. "But you are together?"

"Four years in May."

"You're both celibate?" I asked in disbelief.

"Almost four years," she replied quietly as she swept her hands through the sand, grabbed a pile, and cast it away.

I asked Annie if she and her girlfriend had ever made love. She said they had when they first started going out, but her girlfriend never felt right about it because she was straight. I was fascinated by this new and strange scenario. "So why doesn't she see guys?"

"She loves me," she answered as if it were obvious.

"That's pretty unusual," I said trying to hold back a laugh. "So, now what? You're ready to cheat on her? This would be cheating, right?"

"We've decided to have an open relationship."

I hadn't heard the term open relationship since my parents had tried it in the sixties. "That's a bad sign."

Rachel sat up and affectionately grabbed a pillow. "Well, I kind of like Annie. I mean, she sounds really quirky. Have you made love to her?"

"Yeah," I insecurely mirrored her actions. "I had

to fall in love with her first. It took me a couple of weeks."

"I know what you mean. It usually takes me a while. But not with Sandy, the woman I'm kind of seeing now. She's an athlete, too." Rachel drifted off. "Sandy has the best lats I've ever seen. She's a beautiful Asian woman, tall and sensually muscular like a tennis player, not a body builder. I met her the first night I set foot in the bar. She asked me out on a date, but I didn't tell her I was married. I didn't want to scare her. Anyway, we did go out a couple of times before I told her about my husband."

"She drove us up to the top of Mulholland." I shrank a little remembering I had taken her to Mulholland earlier in the night. I have to find new places. "We parked and looked out over the city. She said she'd wished I'd told her about being married sooner. She said she wouldn't have gotten involved with me if she had known. Then Sandy went into this tirade about how she'd come to a point in her life where drama was a real turnoff. She said she was sorry, but she just didn't have the desire to get involved with me; that it seemed unhealthy."

Sandy must have been made of wood to turn Rachel down. Rachel was irresistible. "What did you say to her?"

Rachel rolled on to her stomach and stuffed two pillows under her chest. She acted as if we had known each other since the sandbox days. I wondered how many people use conversations about exes as foreplay for lovemaking. I held a pillow in my lap shyly and stiffened as she spoke.

"I told Sandy I didn't think it would be such a big deal. I was getting a divorce. I didn't even sleep in the same bed with him. Sandy wasn't impressed; she said we shouldn't make love until I worked out my problems first. So I played it cool and told her to just let me give her a massage. She let me rub her back for a while and then suddenly turned around, grabbed my face, pulled me down in her lap, and kissed me wildly."

"I can't handle this," I said as I playfully slugged my waterbed. "I get jealous of things that happened before I knew you, and I don't even love you." Rachel gazed at me compassionately. Did she feel the same thing or was it wishful thinking?

"Your turn," she said once again rolling over, fidgeting to get comfortable and ending up on her side.

"Pee break?" I asked

"Pee break," she repeated, hopping off the bed and prancing down the hall to the bathroom. I squirmed around my bed and tried to look casual. Oh god, I hope the bathroom's clean. What if she looks in the shower and sees the tar bubbling up from the drain? I have to get that fixed. Why is there tar coming up from my shower?

Rachel walked back to the bedroom and pounced on the bed. "You?"

"I have an amazing bladder," I said, regretting the comment instantly.

"So, spill it," she said. At first I thought we were still on the subject of my bladder and I froze. "Oh, okay." I got with the program.

"Destiny, my first straight girl. I first met Destiny around Christmas time. I was shopping for one or two just-in-case presents for anyone I had forgotten.

I'm Jewish, but our family always celebrated the Christmas gift-giving tradition; it's some kind of California Jewish phenomenon.

"Anyway, I walked out of Urban Outfitters carrying bags of gifts like Santa's Jewish helper, and there parked on the street just like any other car, sat my dream car. This silver Avante is talking to me. It whispers, 'Loretta, I should be your car.' Of course, I stood by it for a minute to pick its brain. Suddenly from behind me, this French female voice yelled 'Get away from my car!' I jumped outta my skin like a cartoon cat. I turn around and behind me stood this thin blond cutie. She was laughing at me in French. I apologized for getting too close to her car. 'Oh, this is not my car,' she said, still cackling. So I asked her if she would like to get some coffee with me and she said, 'Of course.'

"Over the years we became friends. I was attracted to her twisted sense of humor and her great looks, but she insisted she was extremely heterosexual. I gave up any hope of us driving off into the sunset in an Avante with two dogs and a fondue set with all the forks.

"Then years later, she called me. I was at home alone writing about being alone at home. 'Lo,' she says, 'it's Destiny. I'm ready to make love to you.' She rolled her words out like a red carpet. See, that's how it is with those straight girls; 'make love to me'; now she's the aggressor . . . I asked her to what I owed the honor. She said, 'I'm ready to do it. I want to bump and grind with my own self-image . . . I'm dying to feel the flesh of another chick's breasts against my own . . .'

" 'Keep talking . . .' I say, getting into it.

"So Destiny said, 'I really want to do this thing, Loretta, and you're the only lesbian I know.'

"She'd lost me, and I was so close, too. 'Des', I said, 'I can't make love with you now. I need better wooing than 'you're the only lesbian I know.'

"She says she's sorry, that she didn't mean it. She meant to say she's attracted to me . . . and she loves me, as a friend. Then she pleads, 'Come over and seduce me.' "

"Well, did you go and seduce her?" Rachel inquired.

"I didn't see much room for seduction. I can't make love on cue. It has to happen, you know, spontaneously."

"But Destiny persisted. 'Darling . . . it's me, Des. You've wanted me forever.'

" 'Well, not forever.' I said, but it had been forever.

" 'Honey,' Des says working the French accent. 'This is my first, maybe only, time with a woman. I want you to make it fun, please . . .' "

Rachel sat up on the bed and gave my legs a little shake. "So what did you do?"

"I told Destiny the answer was no, I would not come over. I felt weird about the whole thing. Usually I'm the one in control, and she had usurped my power. So, I said no thanks, nice offer and all, but no, and I hung up the phone."

Rachel seemed disappointed to hear I had wimped out with Destiny, but I couldn't tell her the real story without going into the sleazy details. I would have had to tell Rachel how I'd sat around the house for only a few minutes after hanging up the phone with Destiny.

"Des was so sexy she could part a room quicker than Moses. I was driving to her pad, fantasizing about the blond peach fuzz on her upper thighs glistening in the sunlight after being rubbed with oil.

"Des lived in a security building in Hollywood, which was kind of an oxymoron. The front door was always broken; the buzzers didn't work; and her name wasn't listed on the box anyway. I pushed my way inside and walked along the green-stained carpet to the elevator. She lived on the fourth floor, three floors higher than I'd ever consider living on a fault line. I stepped in the elevator, circa 1940, which was more the size of a dumbwaiter or a coffin, but I didn't want to think about that. Her door was directly across the hall from the elevator. When the doors opened I was where I wanted to be. I rang the buzzer even though I was correct in assuming it didn't work. Then, getting into character, I knocked hard three times.

" 'Who is it?' I could hear her muffled voice say as the peephole darkened.

" 'It's your maintenance girl,' I said sounding very butch and preoccupied, just like a maintenance girl would.

"Destiny was no dummy and followed my lead flawlessly. 'Finally,' she said, unlocking her door and opening it wide. 'I called the super days ago. It's my pipes again.' Destiny stood in the doorway with a glass of dry white in one hand and an empty cigarette holder in the other. She was wearing a black silk negligee, fishnet stockings, and blue garters. It looked like she'd started without me.

" 'Did I come at a bad time?' I said, setting down my Indigo Girls lunch pail, the only thing I had that remotely resembled a toolbox.

" 'No, this is perfect, I was just having a glass of wine. Would you like some?'

" 'I never drink on the job. I'll just take a look at your plumbing, if you don't mind.' Destiny shrugged agreeably and went into her bedroom. I took my lunch box into the kitchen, set it on the counter, and went to work. A few minutes later I poked my head into her bedroom. She was sitting reading Anais Nin's *Delta of Venus* in an antique chair, her legs crossed and swaying side to side unconsciously. 'Ma'am', I said as I walked into her room and sat across from her on the bed, 'I've played with your faucets, checked under your sink. There is nothing wrong with your plumbing. You seem fine to me.'

"She unwound her legs and tipped her chair forward. 'Maybe you were just looking in the wrong place,' she said spreading her legs and wrapping them around my waist.

"I gently grabbed her waist and lifted her easily out of the chair. I laid her upper body down on her frilly floral bedspread. Her hips rested on the edge of the bed; her jungle-red toenails whisped across the floor. I stood up between her white thighs dangling off the bed. I dug my fingers into the tiny hole on my T-shirt and ripped it wide open revealing my braless breasts.

"The collar of the shirt remained unscathed, which if she were religious would have added an extra thrill. I guess she had never had the experience of caressing a woman's breasts before, because she attacked them over-zealously. I always had very large breasts, which I thought was a cruel trick for god to play on a dyke. While I was a teenager praying for a flat chest, all the other girls in the world were wishing for big breasts. I'm stuck carrying around other girls' wishes.

"She ran her fingers around my nipples and areolas like a blind archeologist reading braille hieroglyphics. She pulled me against her open mouth and sucked hungrily at my nipples. I let her suck and lick at my breasts until she reached an uncontrollable frenzy. I'd swear her tongue had the surface of a shag rug; it felt scratchy like a welcome mat.

"I pulled away from her and went down on the floor between her legs. I gently ran my teeth up and down her fishnets. I clenched down on the silky material with my two front teeth and pulled them until they ripped. I lifted her calves onto my shoulders and let her watch as I shredded each of her stockings slowly with my mouth. She smiled seductively as I ran my hands up the sides of her thighs ripping material and dropping it on the floor. I grabbed her garters, which were now clipped loosely from her panties to some shreds of fabric. I yanked the garters, and her French-embroidered lace undies followed loyally down her legs. I slid them around her feet and onto the floor.

"I lay on top of her and slid her clingy silk nightie over her head. I still wore my blue jeans with a bulky belt giving a nice white-trash, repair-gal effect. I crawled down her body rubbing my tan breasts against her pale skin. She was sprinkled with a hundred tiny birthmarks from good deeds done in previous lives. I ran my lips around her neck, her small perky breasts, her tall cherry-colored nipples, but at no time did I use my tongue. I plucked at her body with my mouth as if I had nothing inside it. She was writhing around the bed saying things in her native language. I pressed my ribs between her legs, rotating by body all around and teasing her mercilessly. I dry kissed my way between her thighs. I blew warm air against her anxious clitoris. She grabbed my head and pulled me into her. I kept my mouth closed and kissed her pussy a dozen times without my tongue. She started shouting French expletives and digging her nails into my arms. All of which was very exciting but I decided she had suffered long enough.

"I released my tongue inside of her warm peach a little at a time. I'd teased her too much for her to turn back now. Her legs wrapped around me; her hands clutched my hair; her body went into a series of convulsions that almost made me come through osmosis. As she came she pulled my mouth away from her and spasmed with aftershocks. She cried and spoke to me lovingly, but I didn't understand a word; she was speaking in French. That was the first and last time we made love. Soon after, Destiny and I lost touch with one another, though our friendship had never been unpleasant or awkward, just fond memories of a foreign language."

"So what ever happened to Destiny?" Rachel asked curiously.

"Destiny's history," I replied.

"I slept with Madonna once," Rachel blurted out,

trying to top me. I looked at her. She remained uncomfortably silent. "Well, a friend of mine did," she conceded. We both laughed, clearing the sexual tension that was piled almost as high as my clothes.

"I should go now," Rachel jumped up off the bed.

"I'll drive you," I said following her into the living room. Talking about exes can be just like having sex, I thought as I drove Rachel to her car. I wondered if we had gotten to know each other too quickly.

3

It seems like whenever I get my period, I feel like everyone else has it, too. That's why I wanted my cartoon alter ego, Heavy Myrtle, to have her period in one episode. It wasn't like I wanted her to have a period every month. I wouldn't wish that on anyone. It would be her first and last period on the show.

However, this was not just my decision. I had to run it by my writing partner, Noah Rothman.

Noah and I were buddies as well as work partners. Just looking at him made me laugh. He was a cross between an obsessive-compulsive, anal-retentive corporate-executive type and the leader of a guerilla army.

Noah, who stands six two when he's slouching, and I were crowded in my tiny kitchen. I offered Noah an espresso. As usual he said he didn't want one and then drank mine. Some people seem to prefer the taste of food or drinks I have prepared for myself.

"You have to remember who our audience is. They're yuppies, not some radical feminist lesbians." Noah started in on me while I purposely ran the grinder trying to drown him out. I admit it was passive-aggressive, but plain aggression can be far more dangerous in the cartoon business.

Noah opened my refrigerator to rifle through my food. There wasn't enough nonfat yogurt or fat-free muffins in the universe to satisfy a man of his build, so I kindly closed the fridge and directed his attention to my espresso. "Noah." He gulped down a double like it was only a thimbleful, "This is not a lesbian thing. All women have their periods."

"Loretta, no one wants to see a menstruating superhero. It's not funny, it's dangerous." He opened my cabinets discovering an unopened box of matzo.

I snatched the box from his hands and put it back in the cupboard. "All women can relate to it. They need to see themselves and their bodily functions reflected positively in the media."

"Granted. Look, she can have her period, but PMS is out of the question. She could destroy the city." Noah made one last ditch effort to eat some fat-free Fig Newtons I had left out the previous week and appeared triumphant when I didn't stop him.

We walked into my home office. We prefer to

work in a casual space rather than be subjected to the dreaded fluorescent lights and cubical environment we spent years trying to escape.

My office is located in my backyard in a guest house conversion. It has a unique view of overly green grass and an overly blue pool. My gardener and my pool man had a secret plot to take colors beyond reality and knew that if they were to pursue this as an art form they'd have to accomplish it in Los Angeles. The office contained two shelves lined with books and tapes, poster renderings of Heavy Myrtle from our animators, and two desks. Noah had a hot laptop on his, and there was an IBM knockoff on mine. I enjoy the luxury of seeing each sentence I write stretched across a large computer screen. He'd be content writing on a napkin.

We kept a TV monitor and a VCR in a corner of our office so that we could watch our previous shows whenever necessary. The walls were covered with poster prints of various legendary and contemporary females like Amelia Earhart, Fanny Brice, Anne Bancroft, Ingrid Bergman, Helen Reddy, Mae West, Lily Tomlin, and Barbra Streisand. Noah insisted that I hang a picture of Alfred E. Newman for his personal inspiration.

"I just think we should take some risks," I said dipping my foot in the pool before we stepped into the office. The water was refreshingly cold for the summertime. I never understood why people would heat their pools so it felt like they were taking a bath. If you can't shiver and examine your girlfriend's hardened nipples when you hop out of a pool, what's the point?

Noah cued up our latest show on the VCR. "Last

week you had Myrtle cruising the city looking for a lover. That seemed risky."

"Superheroes need love too," I explained.

"Myrtle is a public servant. The audience wants to see her swoop down and help some couple deal with their in-laws' constant badgering. They don't care if Myrtle's gettin' any. She's a couples counselor, not a sex surrogate."

We both sat on the couch in front of the TV. I pressed play on the remote and up on the screen popped Heavy Myrtle. Theme music swelled and receded as we saw Myrtle seated at a restaurant table next to her male date.

"Don't take them to all your favorite restaurants." As soon as she says this, Myrtle notices the man has vanished. "In case they leave you, you'll have somewhere to eat," she rebounds.

She then flies through the air like an albatross. She weaves awkwardly through office buildings and warehouses. She plummets downward, landing hard on her feet, cracking the concrete below, in the middle of a dilapidated, downtown city street.

Myrtle counsels her viewers: "Live like a shark. Keep your eyes wide open. Don't eat, sleep, feel, or show them any signs of being human, and you can have whomever you want, for the rest of your life."

The show ended as I clicked off the tube.

Noah spoke abruptly. "See, Myrtle has to be alone. She has to suffer. That's what makes her funny and insightful."

Secure in my knowledge that my needs and Myrtle's desires were identical, I sounded off. "Some day she will meet someone and fall in love, and she will have a healthy relationship."

"Over my dead body." He crossed his arms as if that closed the subject.

4

Anyone could tell that Little Frida's health food restaurant and coffee house was a quaint little lesbian café. The Frida Kahlo motif was the first clue. Secondly, Georgia O'Keefe paintings adorned the natural wood walls. Third clue: Dykes were swarming the place.

I couldn't decide between the garden burger or the chilled gazpacho, but I was sure I didn't want the walnut salad. I don't like nuts in my food.

Veronica Anne Vance was one of my dearest friends. She was notorious for being late, and this day was no different. When she finally did enter the café, she looked frazzled and confused. I didn't have the heart to reprimand her tardiness. Veronica was about as cute and charming as a woman could be without being a child. Her eyes sparkled with a naivete which could only be attributed to her having lived a sheltered existence. Men were constantly following her in and out of places, often leaving their dates behind. She remained unaffected and almost unaware of the commotion she could create in a single afternoon.

"I'm so sorry I'm late. I thought I knew a shortcut, and I got lost," Veronica said as she set down her gigantic backpack overflowing with books, papers, laptop computer, and a thermos. She took off her purse and set it on the corner of the chair, reached down and rummaged through her backpack, came up with a vitamin container and plunked it down on the table as if to say, I'm ready to begin.

"Hi," I said.

"Hi," she sighed.

Just as we were starting to get cozy the waitress approached us, menus outstretched. Her rainbow-colored name-tag read BREEZE. She was a sexy woman, almost a human version of a black cat. Her black dress with bright red seams clung to her slender body like a second skin. Her neckline plunged, revealing her ample breasts. The erotic way her red stockings crept up her legs leaving only inches of bare skin between her dress and stockings sent a chill across the floor and up my spine. I decided my tactic then and there: I would flirt with her subtly. Anything excessive and I'd lose her interest.

"Hi." Breeze directed her come-on unnecessarily towards Veronica. "Can I get you something to drink?"

Veronica, who was chronically on autoflirt, grinned back at Breeze. "You know, can I have a —" she looked at me for help. "What is that tea that's great for cramps?"

I was about to try to answer her question when the Breeze blew in. "Raspberry herbal tea is excellent for relieving cramps. I swear by it."

I made an exaggerated head whip toward the waitress wondering if she had missed the etiquette course in waitress school or the boundaries session in therapy.

"Really? Great. I'll have some," Veronica said, apparently unfazed by this intrusion.

"Oh, but we don't carry that here." Breeze pondered a solution. "How about a nice chamomile or ginseng?"

"Chamomile would be lovely. And what kind of soup do you have today?" They spoke to each other as if I didn't exist.

The waitress swayed her shoulders forward revealing her cleavage as she spoke. "Oh, we have a delicious vegetable barley soup."

"And there is no chicken or beef bouillon in that?"

Having had quite enough of their foreplay, I decided that it was time to intervene. "It's a vegetable soup."

"No, it's a vegetable base," the waitress reiterated, ignoring me completely.

"And no cheese?" cross-checked Veronica.

Having successfully destroyed the napkin in my lap, I was going to town on the tablecloth with my fork.

"No cheese," wooed Breeze. "It is slightly spicy, though, if you don't mind that."

"You know, I'll just have the dinner salad, no dressing, just some lemon on the side. Thanks."

"You're very welcome," she said, meaning every word of it — and more. The waitress lingered briefly, her eyes fixed on Veronica a few minutes past blatantly obvious. Finally she turned toward me and with an expression of undeserved contempt said, "And what can I get you?"

"I'll have the same with extra ranch dressing on the side, please." I gave her all the attitude I could muster. She curled her lip and turned to walk away as I shoved my coffee cup toward her. "And some squaw bread." She slinked off.

"So how are you?" I said to Veronica as I tried to shake off the bad vibes.

"Well. I'm trying to finish my master's thesis on the neotribal art in America. There has been this whole resurgence of tattoo and piercing fetishes that absolutely fascinates me. I'm still substitute teaching for a class of twenty-four diabolical eight-year-olds, and I don't think their real teacher is ever coming back." She opened her vitamin bottle and filled her hand with a varied assortment of colored pills. "Oh, I finally bought my massage table, so if you know anyone who needs a good Swedish massage, I'm fully licensed. And I've just started installing computer hardware in people's homes . . ." She popped the pills in her mouth, took a big gulp of water to slosh them back, and made a satisfied "ahhh" noise to complete the ritual.

As Veronica elaborated on all the subjects she had just briefly touched upon, it occurred to me she had always followed an outline approach to conversation. When I called her on it she changed lanes and conducted a rapid-fire question-and-answer session. Maybe she's hypoglycemic and needs nourishment to settle her down, I thought as she pulled out a container of carrots and began to snack on them. It fascinated me to watch her eat her own food while waiting to be served at a restaurant. She offered me some carrots and wasn't fazed when I told her I was just about to eat.

When the salads arrived, Breeze had toned down considerably. She was now functioning at a moderate, hard-sell flirt. Veronica casually introduced her carrots onto the plate with the salad. She ate meticulously, making sure her food stayed in her mouth long enough for her salivary glands to begin the digestion process. "Most people swallow their food before they even have a chance to taste it," she explained as she chewed.

In mid-conversation Veronica abruptly pushed her half-eaten salad away from herself. "I'm so full, I'm so fat."

"Did you ever think that maybe your body is firm, but your mind needs some trimming?" She smirked at me, pulled her salad inward, and resumed eating. "You must discuss this in therapy?"

"Well, yes, of course, we discussed it," she confided. "But it's really hard for me to really trust her opinion, you know, 'cause she's overweight."

"You think because she's heavy she can't be objective?" I asked incredulously. "Her weight doesn't effect her vision."

"That's exactly what she said when I pointed it out to her." Veronica materialized a tiny pill bag out of nowhere and swallowed three. "Digestive enzymes," she volunteered. "So, are you still seeing that athlete?"

"Annie. Yeah, but it's on its way out. The other night, though, I met this woman, Rachel, who's pretty exciting to me, but she reeks of unavailability."

Veronica considered my predicament. "I guess I'm pretty lucky to have Douglas. He's so available."

"But do you love Douglas?"

"I don't think love is really the point." She took out the rest of her salad, scooped it into her Tupperware bowl, snapped on the lid, and popped it into her bag. "All the relationships I had in the past failed to work if I loved the guy. So now when I like a guy and think we're fairly compatible, I get together with him and try to decide if I want to marry him. Instead of loving him, I'd rather just get along with him, so I can maintain my freedom and identity and have kids before he leaves me because I'm too independent."

"You're great, Veronica."

"You think so? You don't think I'm too fat?"

"No way," I smiled.

"You're my best friend, Loretta, my very best friend."

"I love you, Veronica."

We were about to have our first moment of connectedness when Breeze came back to the table to rearrange things.

"Can I get you two anything else?" She directed every molecule of her being toward Veronica's big blue eyes.

Veronica appeared to have caught something contagious. "No, thank you." She paused. "That was delicious."

I lunged my body over the table, breaking their Svengali eye sorcery just short of complete hypnosis. "Just the check, please." Neither of them snapped out of the spell. I watched in amazement as they experienced something I have always wanted to feel. It was as if everyone around them didn't exist. We were just Vaseline smeared on their lenses.

"Are you sure? We have this incredible tofuti chocolate mousse."

"Oh, that sounds great, but I'm on a macrobiotic diet."

"Really? I'm on a juice fast!" Breeze trilled.

"I eat whatever I want," I added curtly.

Veronica and Breeze smiled at each other like a couple of Masons who shared a cheap, ancient secret. I wondered where I lost control. Breeze casually wrote the check and dropped it in midair. It floated to the table like a love letter. She then cleared the table, nonchalantly brushing up against Veronica's forearm with her left hand while taking her plate. Veronica's eyes remained transfixed on Breeze even as she disappeared into the kitchen.

"I can't believe what just happened. Have you ever been so sexually stimulated that the muscles inside you . . ." Veronica motioned towards her crotch, ". . . go like this . . ." She rapidly opened and closed her hand in a spasm-type movement demonstrating her internal reaction to this waitress. “I just felt that! I have to make love to that woman.”

“Excuse me? You? Lover of all that is male? Friend to semen? You want to partake in the female love garden?”

“You have to help me get that woman,” she insisted. “I don’t know what just happened, but I had a vision. Venus on a half shell just entered my life.”

Veronica grabbed my arm and looked into my eyes. I stared right back at her, trying to calculate whether her possession was permanent. “Promise me you’ll fix me up with that lesbian,” she pleaded. “I want to make love to a real lesbian.”

“As opposed to a phony lesbian who occasionally fantasizes about men?”

“No, I want a woman who only touches women, a true female diva.”

“I bet you want a femme girl.” I knew from experience, straight girls want femme girls to play with, just like the dolls they had as children. They can dress up, share makeup, take scented baths together, double their high-heel collection, roll on the bed, and play doctor. Their biggest worry, fighting over the mirror before they go out at night.

“Yes, a feminine woman . . . like a dream you awaken from too soon.” She swooned.

“Please, Veronica, you’re scarin’ me.” I grabbed my bag and picked up the check.

“I’m sorry, I just feel so euphoric. Will you get me that lesbian?”

I put down some money for the check and included a reasonable 20 percent for the performance piece. I took Veronica by the arm and escorted her to the door. "I don't even know if she's gay. Besides, I can't just 'get' you a lesbian. They're not like a pair of shoes."

Veronica stopped at the door. She wasn't going to move until she was satisfied. "Well, perhaps some other lesbian goddess then."

I hesitated for a moment. "I could introduce you to a few. If you promise to act human."

"I will, I'll act human." We walked outside as Veronica sniffed the fresh air. "Suddenly I feel so woman-centered."

"Well, that seems healthy enough, being that you're a woman and all."

An attractive girl strolled past us toward the cafe. Veronica checked her out like she was comparing veal in the frozen foods section. "Come on," I said as I dragged her off in the opposite direction.

5

A tropically-colored banner hung above the bar mirror, proclaiming ISLAND NIGHT in large Hawaiian-style lettering. Painted signs flanked the bar, offered drink specials, MAI TAI ONE ON!!, FRU FRU CAN'T HURT YOU, CHI CHI'S, TWO FOR ONE. The mirror was ornately painted with palm trees, tiki torches, and layered chips of mother-of-pearl clouds set aflame against a bloody sunset. Fresh tropical flowers brightened the tables. Every girl in the bar had a coconut drink littered with plastic accoutrements like a twisty straw, a monkey, a mermaid, and a flying dolphin, all trying to escape their coconut prison.

Celia brooded behind the bar in her grass mini, fresh gardenia lei, and a coconut halter top strapped to her with woven banana leaves. Celia never did anything halfway and appeared to be regretting it as she adjusted the leaves digging into her shoulder blades.

Annie, who loved the giant banana leaves on the back wall by the dance floor, sucked the straw of her fruit-blended cocktail like she was sipping drinks in Hawaii. I knew there was a slim chance I could make love to Annie if I didn't broach the subject we had met to discuss. But I couldn't hold back any longer. Seeing Annie swaying to the reggae music and eyeing every chick in the place irritated me into action.

I sat up on the arm of the leather couch. "You know, Annie," I started to say, but she was waving at some girl playing pool. Apparently she couldn't wave and hear at the same time. "Annie," I repeated. She swung her head toward me like she was totally put out. "You tell me you love me, you beg me to spend the night, and then in the morning you treat me like I'm a bad one-night stand."

"I know," she replied without a glimmer of remorse. She set her girl drink down on the papaya-shaped coaster.

"And I know that you've got this psychodrama between you and your girlfriend, and now she calls and wakes me in the middle of the night and screams. I know it's her, so don't tell me it must be one of my exes."

"I know," Annie snickered, obviously reminiscing fondly over her ex's tiny hiney. "It probably is her," she calmly continued. "One time she tried to run me over with her Jeep, but I ran behind a telephone pole, so she hit that instead." Annie got up off the couch. "Look — she even broke two ribs once with a tree branch. She told the paramedics it just fell on me." She lifted her sheer metallic shirt to reveal the lumps from her poorly healed broken bones.

I was too busy admiring the lower halves of her gorgeous breasts to stare idly at relationship war wounds. "See, this is not healthy. She is a very dangerous woman."

Annie sat back down in a huff. "Well, it wasn't all her fault. I kind of provoked her when I pushed her off this embankment, but I didn't mean to hurt her."

"I think you guys should give it a rest. It sounds like a drama binge to me. You should decide if you want to be with me or your invisible limb of a girlfriend."

"Loretta, you know I'm in love with you, but Chauncey is everything to me. I grew up with her, and she's always there for me. If you can't understand that, then maybe we shouldn't be seeing each other."

"Yeah, right, right. You're going to leave me to go back to a girl named Chauncey who never makes love to you but occasionally tries to kill you?" I poked her in the ribs to remind her.

"Don't put her down; you don't even know her." Annie exploded. She started to gather her things, grabbing her pull-out stereo, her cellular phone and her gold Zippo lighter off of the coffee table and shoving them into her big, shiny, electric blue backpack.

"I don't think I'd want to get near her." I stayed still having nothing to gather.

Rachel and Sandy entered the bar and glanced around the room, laughing at the Tahitian hell that Celia had created. Rachel noticed us in the back and subtly pointed me out to Sandy. Then they slowly worked their way over to the table.

"You know, Chauncey and I love each other more than you'll ever experience in your lifetime," Annie stood up with purse in hand just as Rachel and Sandy walked over.

"Hi," said Rachel. She noticed the weird energy. "I'm sorry, I didn't mean to interrupt you. I just wanted to say hi."

I got off the couch since everyone else was standing. "Rachel, this is Annie. Rachel's a friend of mine."

"Hi." Annie stood still, trying not to be too rude.

"This is Sandy." Rachel swung her hand up toward Sandy. "Loretta and Annie. So . . . what are you guys up to?" Rachel attempted to break the tension as she rocked back and forth and smacked her hands together.

Annie was too angry to feign normalcy. "We were just breaking up." She turned to me sharply. "Loretta, don't bother to call me. I'll be at Chauncey's." Annie stormed out of the bar without looking back.

I yelled after her to save face. "Don't bother to call me either I'll be —" I was stopped cold with nothing to say. I turned towards Celia with the only finish I could think of, "— here at the bar."

I collapsed onto the couch, wounded. "What a psycho!"

Rachel sat down and tried to console me. "I'm really sorry. Did you guys have a fight?"

"No. If we had fought, I'd have broken ribs."

Rachel smiled.

"Well, you could always call her at Chauncey's," suggested Sandy. "What is that, a restaurant?" It was obvious the girl had a big heart and needed it for all those muscles.

"No, it's a halfway home for codependents."

Sandy started for the bar. "Rachel, let's say we buy Loretta a shot."

"She'll be back. They always come back a few times just to make you suffer more, if not anything else." Rachel slapped my knee jovially.

I took a deep breath. "Let's get some shots."

Sandy was standing at the bar having no luck flagging down Celia. Celia always played hard to get with newcomers. Regulars got the royal treatment. I was hoping to show Sandy and Rachel some of that special treatment, but Celia ignored me, too, her garb apparently obstructing her movement.

"Hey, Celia, can we get some help down here!" I called down to her end of the bar.

"It's a little late for a brain transplant," she hollered back at me. Then she strolled leisurely down the bar. "Whad'ya need, ladies?"

Celia had heard me and Annie mixing it up and had to put her two cents in the slot. "Loretta, you got off easy. She and her girlfriend would have sapped you dry. I've seen it happen. Hell, I've done it. Never fall in love with half a woman, 'cause chances are the other half is at home designing voodoo dolls."

"C, just a drink, please." I leaned on the bar,

both denying and trying to come to terms with this recent loss. I knew Annie and I would never work as a couple, but I still felt an internal theft had occurred.

Sandy tried to help me. "You can hang out with us; we were just gonna shoot some stick."

"No, thanks. You guys go and have fun. I'll just sit here in the dark. I'll be all right."

"What do you want to drink, hemlock?" Celia countered. She detested martyrs worse than straight couples cruising for a third.

"You got any?" I slumped on the bar as Celia tossed a beautiful orchid lei around my neck. She then began to fix some elaborate drinks with umbrellas and girls on swizzle sticks.

"Ah, Loretta, come on, that girl's average," Rachel said as she hopped onto a stool. "She's great lookin', but she's got no bread in her toaster."

Sandy looked down the barrel of a cue stick to judge if it was crooked. "She was gorgeous. Great definition."

We all looked at Sandy like "Which of those statements did not belong?"

"But she's too tall," she added, trying to recover.

"I thought I loved her. She said she loved me." I looked at my nails. They were in desperate need of a cleaning.

Celia shook a goblet of unknown liquid. "If I had a nickel for every wench that said she loved me, I'd be playing poker on the French Riviera with Princess Di." Celia set out three rocks glasses and poured in her mystery drink. We were all just happy not to have to drink out of a coconut. "Here, try this. It's love potion number ten. One sip of this stuff will make you recognize your one true love, and you won't settle 'til you win her over."

I held my glass to the light trying to see what was in it. Rachel and Sandy followed suit thinking I was about to say a toast, so I did. "To love potion number ten. Let's hope as I drink it, I'll no longer see Annie." We all sipped our drinks and almost lost them instantly.

"Eyukchh! What the hell was that?" Sandy grimaced. "That was disgusting!"

"It tastes like lighter fluid!" Rachel set down her glass and wiped her mouth with a bar napkin.

"No one ever said a love potion had to taste good. I've been trying to get rid of that liqueur for months." Celia wiped down the bar.

"Oh, nice how you off your bad hooch on your friends," I said reprimanding Celia.

"At least it was free." Sandy took another tiny sip from the liqueur.

I nudged Rachel. "Notice how C refrained from joining us on that round."

"Yeah, she's like the leader lemming that doesn't really jump off the cliff." Rachel glanced toward me for backup.

"Right. At the last minute it grabs on to an overhanging branch while the others fall to their doom," I added excitedly as my eyes locked on Rachel. We both laughed. "I can't believe you know about lemmings."

"What's so special about a suicidal rodent?" Celia remarked sarcastically.

Rachel and I smiled at one another. "Wait, I

think I feel that love potion working . . . I love you guys." I glanced at Celia and Sandy, and landed on Rachel.

"I think it's working, too . . ." Rachel gazed back at me.

Sandy took another swig. "I don't feel a thing."

6

Rachel and I talked late into the night. Sandy had fallen asleep at the table after having danced for hours. Sandy could dance better than most people fuck. We broke into a sweat just watching her rip up that dance floor like a gay boy on ecstacy. Kimba and I were laying bets on how long Sandy could remain standing after her dance marathon. Kimba won with her five-minute estimation. Sandy's body lay sprawled across our table. She was now clad in Celia's grass mini, numerous leis, and a straw hat.

Rachel and I sat on either side of Sandy's exhausted body.

"What is it you always wanted to do, all your life?" Rachel asked as she twirled Sandy's hair in her fingers.

"All my life? . . . I always wanted to live a life of high spirituality, . . . eating only what I grew in my own garden." I began to play with Sandy's hair as I had another thought. "Either that or I wanted to make a lot of money and live in a large house with a security gate."

Rachel shook her head agreeably. "You'd think there'd be a happy medium."

"Yeah . . . making lots of money as a spiritual advisor." I looked at my watch, quarter to two. After two A.M. there are only two kinds of people on the road, drunks and cops. Luckily I was neither. It was time to hit the road. "Hey, Rachel, you need a ride home?" I asked.

"I rode my bike." She took the last few swallows of her Evian.

"You can't ride your bike home; it's late. Come on, lemme give you a ride." I got up and stretched my legs until my knees cracked.

"No, I'll be fine. I do it all the time."

"What about her?" I patted Sandy on the back, but she was in the thick of REM sleep.

"I don't think she'll fit in my basket," Rachel joked.

Kimba, who was making the rounds cleaning tables and getting ready to close, overheard our conversation. "I'll give her a ride." Kimba leaned down and whispered something to Sandy.

We walked out the front door. Rachel's Schwinn

mountain bike was chained to a fence alongside the club. Rachel started to unlock it. Her bike wouldn't fit in my car, but I wasn't going to let her drive home in the middle of the night without an escort. "Can I just follow you home?" I squeezed her tires for lack of anything else better to do.

Rachel mounted her bike. "If you can catch me." She gave me a sexy wink and took off down the street.

The race was on. I ran to my car, unlocked the door, and jumped in the driver's seat like Speed Racer. I slipped the key in the ignition which immediately set off my car alarm. I hit the alarm kill button, got the car in gear, turned on 4 Non-Blondes "What's Up," and I burned off and squealed down the road after Rachel.

I looked down side streets and alleys — she wasn't anywhere to be seen. Finally I caught a glimpse of her as she cut sharply around a corner and headed up a small, winding road in the Hollywood Hills.

Rachel smiled and began to pump harder on the pedals when she saw me pull up beside her and pass her. She stood up on her bike and struggled to catch me. I turned up the volume of the music so she could hear the tunes. I kept my eyes on her in the rearview mirror, slowing down to her speed but staying ahead of her to taunt her. She looked exhausted. Finally, Rachel got off her bike and began to walk the bike toward my car. I stopped and watched as she approached. Neither of us said a word. The air was still and the moon was a crescent. The music blared into the night.

She reached my car and got on her bike. She planted one hand firmly on the car's door frame inside the window, and I began to drive. Together we gently rounded a turn. Rachel hung on with her clenched hand. At the next bend she lost her grip and separated from my car. I extended my left arm as far as I could reach and we quickly locked hands. I pulled Rachel up the hill as she pumped the pedals. The music crescendoed. Suddenly Rachel let go of my hand, waved sweetly, and broke away toward her house.

I stopped driving, sat up against my seat back and yelled after her, "Hey, can I see you tomorrow?!"

She hit the brakes and stood holding her bike. "What time?

"Nine o'clock . . ." Rachel smiled approvingly and started to ride off.

". . . in the morning!" I shouted as she dipped down a driveway and out of sight.

7

There's something inherently romantic about having a picnic while hiking in the hills. You could be all alone and you'd still feel loving as you opened the basket after a long day's journey. I once made a rule never to take a potential lover to a place that was special in my heart. I figured if we ever fought and ended up not speaking again, it could ruin that special spot forever. I felt like breaking this rule. I trusted Rachel and wanted to let her see me in what I considered to be my natural habitat.

Rachel and I went hiking in the Hollywood Hills

at our agreed meeting time of nine A.M. I carefully packed a basket with seedless green grapes, a few ripe oranges, a little brie, a loaf of fresh sourdough, and plenty of bottled water.

Rachel's garb was homegirl casual. She wore practically the same long shorts and shlumphy T-shirt I had on. The Hollywood Hills were green and lush with vegetation on that early summer morning. It was slightly overcast, so there was a wet feel in the air. We could smell the mist off the eucalyptus trees, which made huge crackling noises as we passed.

I showed Rachel, who was new to these parts, the poison oak. One mistaken swipe against its leaves and a few days later an itch develops that spreads if you scratch it. It's a very clever plant because it camouflages its vines under and in the midst of other foliage. Its leaves turn dark red in the middle of summer, which means it's ready to do maximum damage to the skin. I asked Rachel to point out any oak she saw, just to make sure she could spot it.

We climbed steep hills over jagged boulders until we found a small waterfall that led to a running creek. "So why'd ya marry him?" I asked as we hopped along stones in a mossy creek bed.

Rachel took a long leap across the water running between two big rocks. "He was a prince . . . and I wasn't *out* yet. Not even to myself."

Rachel tossed her blanket down on a grassy area overlooking the valley. I broke out the oranges. We simultaneously peeled them. "I had it all planned." Rachel tossed her one whole perfect peel in the basket. I struggled and dug into my orange, juice running down my hand. She noticed and gave me a napkin. "I was going to be an accomplished actress married to an accomplished actor, like the Fairbankses but younger. He was my shot at conformity."

"Yuppiedom." My orange was mangled.

"A Suburu station wagon."

"Sunday picnics in the park with your four children with names that rhyme." I took a bite of the whole orange.

"Tommy, Johnny," Rachel paused to think.

"Lonny," I added.

"And Justin." She smiled as she put another perfect section in her mouth.

"Justin?" I wiped the juice from my mouth.

"I always wanted to name my kid Justin."

"I love you . . ." I paused, wanting to strangle myself. "I mean, I love you. Just like that, it slipped out. Shit . . . See how easy it is? When you really feel it, it comes right out. Is that okay?"

Rachel looked into my eyes, her mouth filled with orange. "I love you," she innocently answered. Then she began to chew again and looked away shyly.

8

Like two kids home from the beach, Rachel and I ended up in my bathroom stripped down to our bras and boxers before we had the opportunity to become self-conscious. I turned on the shower as she hopped up on the sink counter and watched me adjust the water. I kept thinking, don't think. I took off my bra, tossed it at Rachel and jumped in the shower while still wearing my black Calvins.

I could see her through the shower door. She looked like an impressionist painting. She opened the door wearing nothing but her thin, white, oversize boxer shorts. She hopped in and closed the door.

We just stood still staring at each other, water pulsated down her sexy buoyant breasts, down her dark strong stomach. Her now-translucent boxers sucked up against the deep black hair that played between her legs. Lucky boxers.

We both stepped out of our skivvies, flung them over the shower door, and began to soap each other silly. We didn't kiss, and we didn't do anything overtly sexual. We were both welling up with a furious passion, which only our shyness contained.

After our shower I lit a fire. We sat watching the cinders turn blue and our faces turn redder. Rachel was wearing a silk kimono which an old friend had left at my house before she moved to Europe. Rachel seemed made for silk and for oversize boxers. She smiled at me and gave a tug on my terrycloth robe's belt.

I never had a problem kissing or making love to a woman before, but Rachel had me scared to passivity. Normally I'd just put on airs. I'd become the perfect lover, the aggressor, the wolf. Instead I sat there dying to kiss her but needing it to be perfect. It seemed we both felt this same dilemma.

I stoked the fire with an iron rod. This was the beginning of something. We both knew it. We sat frozen in front of a flaming fire. "Let's just end this relationship right now." I said sarcastically. We started laughing and fell to the rug, rolling over each other and wrestling playfully. Her cheek swept across my lips. Her hair flung against my face, spreading the sweet scent of her freesia lotion around my body.

Rachel gently rolled me on my back. She held me down and lowered her lips onto mine. We kissed for the first time. Her big juicy lips sucked against my mouth until I could feel my whole soul slipping in and out of her body. She laid her entire weight on me as we tongued each other furiously. I could feel her legs between mine, setting off a bumble bee buzzing inside my box.

She untied her kimono and ran her right hand up my thigh and flung open my robe. She wedged her legs between my thighs and spread them wide. She mounted me and rode me, rubbing her clit against mine in rhythmic jolts. Her hands swam the length of my body sending me into erotic shock. We both moaned in harmony as she twisted and turned all over me. She looked down at me and her hair surrounded my face like a rasta tree engulfing me. We traveled through the rough white waters of intimacy, tumbling breathlessly, and finally emerging to the blue water waves of ecstasy. We came together screaming, which sent us into a fit of uncontrollable laughter. Sex is so much better with a partner.

9

Noah and I were in our office working on a Heavy Myrtle episode about a sophisticated British couple with relationship problems. Mainly, one wanted the relationship, one didn't.

"Darling, don't you think it's time we move in with one another?" I said, spontaneously creating dialogue for the female character, Rhonda.

"Why is it that whenever I kiss a woman they set off to apartment hunting. And making love induces visions of marriage?" said Noah, acting out Larry's part as he typed.

"That's absolutely ridiculous."

"Rhonda, if we move in together now, we shall break up shortly over something petty."

"Larry, if we don't join forces now, I might as well be seeing other people."

Rachel appeared and peeked her smiling face into the office. Noah and I continued to work, incorporating her into the action.

"Rhonda, there is an incredibly large woman making faces at us through the window."

"Larry, do you know who that is? It's Heavy Myrtle. Don't let her in," I screamed, still in character.

"Honey. She is good. And she works for free."

"She's free? All right. But only for a little while."

Noah brainstormed for ideas. "Myrtle struggles through the window and s-a-y-s . . . what does she say?"

"She says," I crouched down and acted like I was climbing through a window, "Hi, I'm Myrtle. You've got fifty minutes."

Noah stopped typing and leaned back in his chair. "Hi, Rache."

"Hi, you guys."

"Hi, honey." I put my arms around Rachel and gave her a kiss.

Noah squirmed slightly. "Ah shit," he said, looking at his watch. "I didn't realize how late it is. I gotta meet that girl."

"What girl?" I called his bluff, thinking he was trying to escape.

"You know, that girl I've been seeing, the one with the abandonment issues."

"That could be any girl."

"I didn't mean to disturb you guys," Rachel said.

"No, you didn't. I really have to split, I have a date with Jolene, the beautiful redhead. How are you, Rache?"

"I'm great! I just got a commercial!"

"Rache, that's great!" I gave her another, even fonder kiss.

"Yeah, that's super."

"I can't believe it. It was my fourth callback. They gave me every test but a pap smear."

"I never even got a call-in on my own movie," moaned Noah. "I woulda been happy with a pap smear."

"Oh, sorry," empathized Rachel.

"No, it's cool. Hey, congratulations, really."

A light wind had finally kicked up in the backyard. A few leaves spun through the air chasing each other in circles, reminding me of something, but I couldn't place it. We walked Noah to the front door.

"Are you sure you can't stay and have some coffee?" I asked him as he exited.

"No thanks, she'll kill me if I'm late . . ."

Noah and I looked at each other and spoke at the same time. I was reading his mind. ". . . Abandonment issues."

Noah left. I turned around to see Rachel standing in the middle of my living room looking like she belonged there more than anything in the house. I wanted her to stay with me forever.

"I am so proud of you, Rachel."

"Yeah? Me, too."

"You won't ever change will you?"

"It's only a hair commercial. I'm not gonna

change." Rachel moved her body into a homegirl stance. "I'm down wid it. I'll still be your homey from the Bronx, G." She dropped the accent and became serious. "And look who's talking. You are gonna be famous in about two days."

"I'm a rock. I can't change." I brought my hands up and rested them on Rachel's shoulders. "Just don't leave me 'cause you get famous, okay?"

"All right. I'll wait 'til I'm washed up."

My eyes saddened. She saw my reaction. "I'm kidding, I'm kidding," she said, embracing me.

We kissed each other while my mind swam with confusion at the prospect of what I was about to say. I wanted to make sure I was coming from the right place. But how do you know what the right place is? It would have been easier for me to say it would make sense for us to move in together for financial reasons than for me to admit that I needed her. I shouldn't need her, I should just desire her as a great addition to my life.

"Rachel, I want you to move in with me."

"Really?"

I tried to read her thoughts, but it was no use. All I could hear were my own insecurities. I kept fearing she'd sense I was asking out of my own need to be loved, and that was selfish.

She took me by the hand and led me to the couch to sit down. I figured she was preparing me for the worst.

"You know, Loretta, if we were to move in together, there is one thing I'm completely adamant about . . ."

I looked at my nails. "I'll clip 'em!"

Rachel held my gaze. ". . . Monogamy. If you ever cheat on me, even just a little, I'll leave you."

"How could I cheat on you just a little?"

"I am totally serious about this," she said. "My father cheated on my mother for years, and it ruined her."

"Okay, okay, Jesus. I feel guilty, and I haven't even done anything. I've never cheated in my life. Well, once I cut school for the day, but it was National School Cut Day, so everybody did it."

10

Renting a U-Haul truck to move is a sure way to jinx a relationship, but Rachel didn't know the joke and had rented one before I could tell her.

The only thing worse than unpacking has to be carrying the obligatory futon. There is no easy way to carry a futon. They are heavy, unwieldy, and should only be used to sleep on as a last resort. We rolled it, roped it, and stashed it in the garage until such time as I could talk Rachel into getting rid of it.

The item of Rachel's which surprised me the most

was the giant picture in the distressed wood frame. Greta Garbo, hair pulled back, dreamy eyed, with lashes so long you could hang Christmas ornaments on them.

"I never knew you liked Garbo." I sat down on a box of books and watched her unwrap the picture.

"I love her. She possessed the full range of being." She stood up and launched into a German accent as she began imitating Garbo. "She was deep, so full of longing, so beautiful, and yet so sad." Rachel changed, becoming Garbo, exaggerating every movement. She pretended she was speaking to a lover across the room. "If you must leave, just go. I'd rather have you leave than regret staying. " She stood alert, yet saddened, in full concentration. "Just go, leave me." She fell to the floor. "Please don't go, I didn't mean it. I need you to stay. Don't leave me. Darling, please, please stay."

I was awestruck by her performance. She had successfully captured the essence of Garbo. I jumped up and applauded her.

Rachel rose slowly from the floor and took a modest bow.

11

There is something thrilling about lying on a bed with your head where your feet should go, especially after having made love in that same defiant position. Rachel stood on the bed frame with one hand poised against the wall to steady herself. I watched her cast a giant shadow against the wall behind her. She finally snagged the wire on its hook and adjusted the Garbo picture above the bed.

"Do you think I'm gay?" she asked casually.

I gazed up at her, suddenly considering that I might have moved too hastily with Rachel. I didn't know if I should dignify the question with an answer so I remained silent.

She was serious. "How do I know?"

"You just know, that's all. It's like being French. Either you are, or you're not."

Rachel dove on top of me. "Put your arms around me and tell me you love me."

I stretched my arms wide and let them fall tightly around her. "I love you."

"You do?" she asked playfully.

"You're a nut."

She whispered in my ear. "And you are a goddess." An electric current traveled from my inner ear through the length of my body, setting off a burning charge between my thighs.

Rachel slowly began to trace the route of the current with her mouth, running her lips around my thin cotton tank top and zeroing in on my nipples, then gently gnawing on them through the fabric. She bit at my ribs through my shirt, ran her teeth around my stomach, and nibbled on my hipbone through my boxers. Goose bumps exploded across my arms and down my legs. I shivered from within, dying for her to satisfy me. She squiggled her body down me, cozily positioning herself between my legs, her feet kicking happily above her. Her mouth pressed firmly on my crotch, puffing her warm breath against my shorts. She slipped her long tongue through the slit in my shorts, parting my lips and darting her tongue in and out of me. A sudden ripple coursed through me and made me shake like a sheet flapping in the wind. I came so fiercely I nearly passed out. Rachel continued licking me until I finally stopped shaking. She looked up at me and smiled with pure love radiating from her eyes. "I'm a lesbian," she said affirmatively.

12

Club 22 was lit like never before. Key lights beamed down on each table revealing scores of hats of all different origins, styles, sizes, and color. There were dayglow colored sombreros, straw hats, top hats, fedoras, sequin-covered tiaras, baseball caps, and a motorcycle helmet. Several women seated at the bar were wearing another varied assortment of clown hats, British police hats, bandannas, and one pith helmet. A woman sitting alone at the corner of the bar wore a dunce cap, which I thought was an interesting choice.

Veronica was a bit perplexed by the hats. I tried to explain to her they had nothing to do with lesbianism — it was just another attempt on Celia's part to generate business with theme nights, like Tracy had suggested. Club 22 was struggling. The large, event-oriented, twice-a-week, posh nightclubs were taking business away from the smaller hometown clubs and causing them to go out of business at a rapid rate. As funky as they were, Celia's theme nights were a creative solution. They gave the bar a much needed makeover.

I pushed Veronica all the way from the entrance clear through to the bar. She was excited about going to a lesbian club. She had even begged me to take her. But as soon as we hit the front door her legs wouldn't bend. Everyone gets shy the first hundred times, I assured her.

Kimba was chatting it up at the helm of the bar. She greeted us by tipping her black cowboy hat, which was punctuated by a circle of bright blue peacock feathers. "Hey, Lo, how's it goin'?" Kimba reached under the bar, pulled out a sailor hat and positioned it on my head.

"Great, how's by you?" I took the hat off and tossed it on the bar.

Kimba took the hat and threw it back where it came from. "I could complain, but what kind of bartender would I be?"

"An average one." I took a quick glance down the bar to see who was in attendance.

"Veronica, this is my friend Kimba."

Veronica offered her hand for a shake. "Oh, the white lion. A pleasure."

Kimba gave her a slow seductive shake. "Likewise."

"Veronica, here, is lookin' fer a femme woman," I said in a southern accent, trying to discourage Kimba from advancing any further.

"Well, you've come to the right place. 'Less, o' course, yer a guy." Kimba eased up, considering she hated to think of herself anywhere south of butchville. "So you say you want a femme girl —" Kimba interrupted herself when she saw Tracy. "— another drink, Tracy?"

"Hey, Trace, I didn't see you." I gave her a hug.

"Oh, great, I'm here so much I'm starting to blend in with the decor."

Tracy wore a blinding Yellow-Cab cap that only accentuated her bleached blond, almost yellow, hair.

"Tracy, this is my friend Veronica. We're trying to round her up a —" Veronica poked me in the rib with her finger and stopped me cold.

"Nice to meet you, Tracy." Veronica's eyes sparkled. "I was just telling Loretta and Kimba I'm looking for women to join a female encounter group for women who want to gain empowerment through getting in touch with their own femaleness."

"Well, I'm just starting to get in touch with my own maleness." Tracy smiled. "Kimba, I'll have another club soda." Tracy winked and leaned one motorcycle boot up on the footrail.

"You don't drink?" asked Veronica.

"No, I'm six years sober." Tracy smacked her gum and fired up a hand-rolled cigarette.

"I think that's so commendable. Congratulations."

"Well, thank you, Veronica." Tracy locked eyes with Veronica, melting noticeably.

"I'll have a club soda, also, please, Kimba," chimed Veronica.

"Veronica hasn't had a drink for over a year," I explained. "She just stopped, cold turkey."

"Well, I like to quit things periodically so they don't become a habit," Veronica offered.

"Like eating?" I whispered in Veronica's ear. She elbowed my rib cage, never dropping the smile on her face.

"So, where are you from, Tracy?" Veronica asked.

"I'm from South Carolina."

"Oh, really? I like your accent. It's kind of tough and romantic at the same time."

Kimba and I stood there, dumbstruck by the spectacle of two greenhorns picking up like pros. "So — you want a beverage, Loretta? I'll join ya."

"Yeah, sure, Kimba." I gave a tug on Veronica's arm. "Can I talk to you a second, Veronica?"

"Sure." Veronica threw a quick, just-a-minute gesture to Tracy as I dragged her over to the pool tables.

"What's the problem?" Veronica picked up a pool ball and began to toss it from hand to hand.

I snatched it from her and set it free on the table. "I hate to burst your water, but Tracy is not a femme. In fact, Tracy makes my Dad look prissy."

"Well, I find her attractive," cooed Veronica as she intercepted a wink from Tracy.

"She is not the earth goddess type. She won't sing songs of joy and dance naked under the moon chanting verses of female empowerment."

"I don't care. I'm enchanted by her androgyny." She looked over toward Tracy again.

"She wouldn't be caught dead using the word enchanted. She's a dyke."

"Is there something wrong with that?" Veronica replied condescendingly.

"Of course not. I'm a dyke. It's just that she drives a Harley. You know . . ." I looked for a response but Veronica was honeymooning in her own little dream world. "She's very learned in the ways of lesbianism. She could overpower a straight girl like you."

"Loretta, just because I am new to this does not mean I'll be demolished. But I appreciate your concern. And," Veronica said as she turned heel and sashayed back towards Tracy, "I love Harleys."

I followed her to finish what I was saying. "I'm just tryin' to look out for you. You know, you might want to just start with a few femme girls . . ." I looked up. We were nearly at the bar. Tracy and Kimba had heard it all and stared at me disapprovingly.

"I was tellin' her something. What?" I groaned.

"Your drink, babe." Kimba shoved a shot of Stoli with a hint of cran my way.

"You wanna play some pool, Veronica?" Tracy said, ignoring me completely.

"I'd be delighted." Veronica flashed a glare at me. Then she smiled sweetly to Tracy. "And call me Nicky."

Tracy extended her open arm. Veronica latched on, and they strolled off to the poolroom.

I turned to Kimba. "Next thing you know they'll be driving Tracy's Harley to Vegas to get hitched."

We raised our shots for a toast and clinked glasses.

"Gee ha." Kimba tipped her hat up, and we both looked off toward the poolroom.

Someone caught Kimba's eye. "Hey, Lo," she said, "I think the one that counts just walked in."

Rachel was standing by the entrance wearing a baseball cap on backward. My heart took a dive for my toes every time I saw her. I'd been marinating in love. I got up from the bar and gave her a hug, burying myself in the fresh scent of her shirt. She smelled like she'd been mixed in a bowl with flour and vanilla. Rachel always smelled clean, even after a daylong hike, even after a sweat-drenched night of sex.

"Hi, sweetie."

"Hi, baby." Rachel put her hands around my neck, gave me a full-mouth kiss, and tucked my tag back in my shirt. Shirt tags jump up my neck constantly.

"Well, hey, girlfriend. How you holdin' up, livin' with Miss Thing?" Kimba leaned forward, hoping for some dirt and getting some.

"It's working out, although we haven't even fought yet."

"Haven't fought yet? Girls, what you been doin'? Makin' love all the time?"

"We talk a lot." I said.

"Well, I know *you* do. So, what would you ladies like to drink this evening?"

"I'll have a light beer," said Rachel.

"Sounds good to me." I looked at Rachel and

wondered why I was standing in a bar when I could be home with her.

The girl in the dunce hat slipped some quarters in the jukebox. A lethal tune, "All About Evil" by The Ringling Sisters, started to fill the bar. As though on cue, J.R., who was the very incarnation of that song, strutted into the club. This woman didn't belong in the white cowboy hat she wore. Her face was too sinister and foreboding. She was tall, dark, and slender. If you didn't know better, you'd have sworn the Marlboro ad girl had just fallen off her billboard.

J.R. caught a glimpse of Rachel and, like a hawk on a hunt, swooped on in for the kill.

Kimba spotted her approach and prepared for the onslaught of talons. "Hi, what can I get you?" Kimba coolly inquired.

"I'll have a shot of tequila with a beer back. And whatever this lovely woman would like." The stranger smiled at Rachel.

Rachel and I looked at each other with disbelief.

"Well, depending on the state of chivalry these days, she might prefer her girlfriend to buy her drinks," Kimba shot back.

"Oh, I'm sorry." She looked me over. "I didn't see you. I'm J.R.," she said, holding out her big hand.

I gave it a shake. "Loretta. And this lovely woman is Rachel."

"Pleasure." J.R. reached for Rachel and locked skin, giving her a slow shake complete with dilated eye contact.

"So, how 'bout if we get you a drink?" I said

lightly, knowing full well I have a tendency to suck up to anyone who makes me feel threatened.

"How 'bout if I get you both a drink?" J.R. tipped her hat like some corny cowboy in an old western.

"Okay, sure. I'll have a shot of what you're having. How about you, Rache?"

"Sure, I'll have the same."

J.R. slapped a twenty on the bar. "So, how long have you two been together?"

I slipped an arm around Rachel's waist. "Since we were five."

"Be nice." Rachel pulled me closer and spoke to J.R. "We've been living together for two months."

"Well, that's great. You guys probably haven't even fought yet," J.R. grinned.

"What is that supposed to mean?" I retaliated.

Kimba set down the drinks. "Here ya go."

"Just an expression," offered J.R. "A toast — to Rachel and . . ." She snapped her fingers as if trying to remember.

"Lo-ret-ta." I overly enunciated each syllable.

"Lo-ret-ta," she said mockingly. "May all your dreams come true." She cocked back her shot. "And all of mine, too," she said as she sucked it down.

"So, what's your story, J.R.?" I said, hoping to draw her out and squash her like a bug.

"Well, I'm in the police academy. I'll be a police officer in one month."

"How unfortunate," I mumbled.

"I suppose you don't like cops?"

"No, not since a couple of good ol' boy types harassed me and called me a dyke for sitting in a parked car and talking with a friend."

"Well, I can't apologize for all police, but you know we've gotta have 'em."

Rachel squeezed my arm. "Not all cops are jerks, Loretta."

"That's right. Some are just like me," smiled J.R.

"Well, that's a relief." I could feel my blood flow constricting, my palms moistening, and my muscles becoming tense.

"So what do you do, Loretta?"

"I'm a writer."

"Oh, yeah? What are you, a poet who doesn't know it?"

I've written poetry for years and have always hated that expression. "What is it with you?"

"I know a poem." J.R. cracked her knuckles. I prepared myself for Dickenson or Plath. "How many police officers does it take to screw in a lightbulb?"

"That's not a poem. That's a joke."

"Most poetry is." J.R. grinned. Round one. "So, how many police does it take to screw —"

"It should only take one, but they have to use all their force," I said flatly.

"That's not how it goes," gloated J.R. "They *want* to use all their force."

I felt like I was regressing to adolescence. I turned to Rachel. "You know, I'm gonna go see how Tracy and Veronica are doing." I gave her a kiss. "I'll be right back."

Breathing deeply, I walked into the poolroom just in time to see Celia placing a Russian fur hat on Veronica's head.

"Hey, how's it going?" I asked.

"I am having such a good time with Tracy." Veronica fiddled with her hat until it sat lower on her head.

Tracy kept her eyes on Veronica while leaning on her pool cue. "Yeah, Nicky was just telling me about uh — what the hell was that? — oh yeah, female mythology. She's very funny."

"Oh, so are you," said Veronica coyly.

I was in no mood for this, either. "Well, I guess I'll leave you two alone," I said and started to head for the bar. I was stopped by Veronica's grip on my arm.

"No, it's fine; what's wrong?" she asked.

"Oh, it's stupid. I'm just getting jealous of that chick over there talking to Rachel."

Tracy, Veronica and Celia looked over toward the bar to catch sight of J.R.

"Why don't you go join them?" Veronica said as she set her cue down on the table. "Or tell Rachel you want to leave."

"Because I don't want her to think I'm jealous."

Tracy patted me on the back. "C'mon, relax and hang out with us."

Veronica gave me a nudge indicating I should try again. "Look, she's really no threat to you. Why don't you go over there and try to be friends with her? We'll be right here if you need us."

I walked back to the bar to catch the tail end of J.R.'s scintillating story.

". . . so we were four-wheelin' up on the ridge, and

they caught up with us and pulled us over. I told him I was almost a cop. He took my beer and said I was almost a criminal, too, but he let us go."

Rachel laughed and leaned in on the bar towards J.R., obviously enjoying the inane banter.

I pressed up against Rachel on the side J.R. wasn't occupying. "So you wanna take off, Rachel?"

"Well, I guess, if you want to." She looked over at J.R. "J.R. was just tellin' me some funny stuff about the police academy."

I couldn't believe Rachel's halfhearted response. "Yeah, well, you can stay if you want. I just would kind of like to get home. We have to get up early tomorrow."

"I don't. I'm having fun. Let's just hang out for a little while and play some pool with J.R." Rachel held my arm gently, but I pulled back. She shrugged and wandered off to the pool tables with J.R.

Kimba rang up a tab and watched me in the bar mirror. She turned around and gave me an understanding nod. I responded with an affirmative shake as we both looked toward the poolroom and then back at each other. "Is this my relationship with Rachel, or is it every relationship I've ever had?"

I gazed around the bar. I was the only girl without a hat.

13

A self proclaimed psychic once advised me never to drive angry, but when I'm angry I forget everything. I was driving a little too fast, but Rachel didn't say a word until I whipped the car into the driveway.

"What is with you? Do you get like this whenever the moon is full?"

"No, that has nothing to do with it. I got jealous! What did you expect? She was touching you, and you weren't stopping her!"

We got out of the car, and I slammed my door hard and wished I hadn't.

"She only touched me for a few seconds. What'd ya want me to do, pull her hands off me?!"

"I took psychology in college." I unlocked the front door, pushed my way inside and threw on the living room light. "I know that touching for three seconds is sexual! You could have politely asked her to get her goddamned hands off you. Christ, I shouldn't have to tell you this!"

"Well, you didn't have to insult her!"

I sat down in my big overstuffed club chair and attempted to remove my boots. "I didn't insult her."

Rachel signaled me to give her my leg. I raised my foot. She grabbed the left boot and vented her anger by yanking it right off. "You told her she had the intellect of Rambo."

"She took it as a compliment."

"That's because she loves Rambo. But you were putting her down." She went for my other boot seeming to almost enjoy the struggle it gave her.

"She's a cop, for chrissake!" I reminded. "A dyke cop. How typical."

"She's not a cop, she's just in the academy."

"She's an aspiring cop. She wants to kill people! What kind of ambition is that? Not serve society and protect — you know, however that goes — she wants to reduce the population!"

Rachel got the boot off and slammed it to the floor. "I know. So she's a little misguided. But I like her. She's funny."

I got up and walked into the bathroom to brush my teeth and get ready for bed. Rachel followed me.

"I'm not saying you have to like her, but I like her, so please try to respect that. She might be a friend. I haven't made many friends since I moved here."

I squeezed out some paste onto my toothbrush. "Oh, and what am I?" I could see Rachel through the reflection in the mirror.

She leaned against the bathroom door, her tone calmer.

"You're my soul mate." Rachel ran her finger along the back of my neck.

"Don't soul mates rank a little higher than potential friends?"

"Soul mates have to put up with soul mates' potential friends."

"Gee, I'm pretty understanding aren't I?" I spit the toothpaste in the sink and rinsed my mouth.

"Yes. Now give me a kiss and tell me why you love me."

I forced a kiss, which made a hollow smack against her lips.

" 'Cause you look great in my wallet."

"Come on, why?" she asked. Her sincerity melted my resistance.

" 'Cause you don't make me feel like I can't eat or sleep or act like who I really am." I ran my hand up her arm and under her sleeve, fingering her luscious creamy skin. "You are bright and beautiful, and you have great skin. And you know the best part about your skin?"

"What?" she sighed.

Her denim shirt tied at the bottom displayed her bare stomach and invited me for a closer look. I untied the shirt, slowly revealing her breasts cupped lovingly in a sheer brassiere. I slid my hand across them so lightly it tickled my hand. "It covers your whole body."

A moment later we were reclining on the bed, Rachel between my legs, me propped against an army of pillows. The love I felt for her at that moment barely fit in the house. If someone had opened the front door, the neighbors would have known. Although this time love had come in the back door. It crept in like a retarded burglar and sat in my closet for months. It is just lucky for love that I ran out of clothes in my A and B closets. What was love thinking, sitting there in a shirt I'd never wear?

So I didn't see it coming. I felt like I had just sunk ten feet deeper and wondered if I'd loved her at all before today.

"So why do you love me?" I asked her, scrounging for the shared experience.

"Well, not for any of the reasons you mentioned. I love you because you're a real friend."

"What does that mean?"

"I love you because I couldn't possibly like you as much as I do without loving you."

"How much do you love me?"

"This much." She spread her arms as wide as she could.

"Is that all?"

"Well my arms are only this long."

I moved her to the side so I could look her in the eyes. "I want you to tell me."

"All right, I love you, well, do you know about the hole in the ozone layer?"

"Yeah," I said, having no idea where she was heading.

"Well, I love you enough to fill that hole."

"Oh, that's romantic. Couldn't you come up with something a little less bleak?"

"That's not bleak, it's hopeful. It's environmentally conscious," she said defensively.

"That's true."

"How much do you love me?" Rachel asked.

"I love you as big as the universe that surrounds our own."

"That's big." Rachel appeared overwhelmed with the enormity of what I'd said.

"It's big love."

I discovered a perfect chocolate chip of a birthmark on her neck and tried to eat it, then another and another. She feigned keeling over from excitement, and I hopped on her back and began massaging her shoulders and her neck.

"You know, it's weird," she said, flipping her hair so I could get more of her neck. "I don't know if you've ever felt like this, but sometimes I feel compelled to tell you I love you 'cause I think I do. But the truth is, sometimes I don't love you. Maybe because sometimes I don't love myself. But even then it's no less disturbing to look over at you loving me and feel nothing. I try not to worry, because I'm sure I will love you later if I can just let it pass."

I slowly lifted my hands away from Rachel's neck so I wouldn't be tempted to do anything rash. "You don't love me all the time?"

"No. Not all the time." She hesitated. "Most of the time, though."

I massaged her again, this time harder. "Oh, good. I thought that it was just me."

Rachel tried to look at me, but I kept rubbing

and she couldn't turn over. "You don't love me all the time?"

"No. Sometimes I don't even like you."

"Yeah, sometimes I hate you."

I pulled away from her and sat upright. "I don't ever hate you."

"Well . . ." she stammered.

"You hate me?" I asked, genuinely offended.

"Not very often."

"But still, hate . . ."

"Hate is pretty strong. Let's say sometimes I loathe you. No, that's worse . . ." She hemmed as she looked for the proper word.

"I get the picture." I crawled under the covers for protection.

She hovered over me. "It's just that, well, I guess I love you like anyone else . . ."

"Intermittently."

"No, like a real person. I mean yes, sometimes I hate you. But I love you enough to hate you."

"You know, sometimes I hate you, too." I rolled over and pulled up the covers.

She leaned up against me and whispered, as though I were sleeping. "You don't have to say that for me."

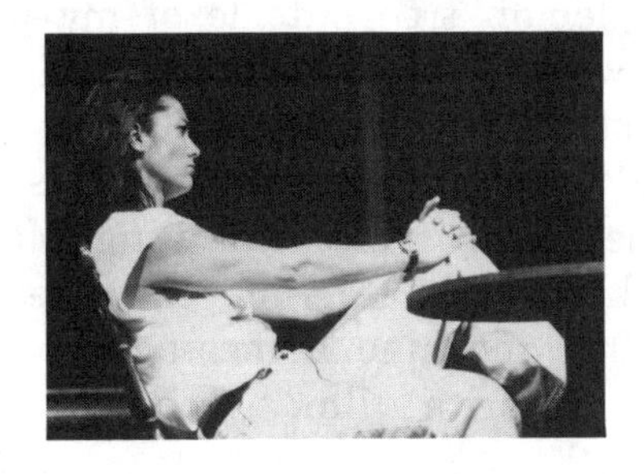

14

I don't care what people say, I can still smell night jasmine during the day. I sat in my office pretending to work while waiting for Noah to arrive. I watched the lemon tree outside of my window as it pretended to work. Oh sure, occasionally it drops a few lemons just to look busy.

The phone rang. I always screen calls to look like I'm busy. I heard my voice imitating Monty Python imitating Shakespeare. "Answer me these questions three and on my machine a message you may leave. What is your favorite film? Who is your favorite actress? And who is your favorite superhero?" The answering machine beeped.

"That's pretty cute, Rachel." Oh, great, it's J.R. Rachel gave her our number. I listened closely in disgust.

"Uh, let's see . . . favorite movie, *The Outlaw Josey Wales;* actress, Sean Young: and super hero, Superman."

Wrong! How could Rachel like a girl like that?

"Oh, it's J.R., by the way. I guess you're off being an actress, huh? Well, give me a call sometime so we can hang out."

What a weasel. But even weasels have their place in the ecosystem. Just as it occurred to me that I should learn to ride a weasel, the doorbell rang.

Noah stood at the front door, bagel bag in one hand and a container of cream cheese in the other, a Jewish writing team cliché.

"Hi. I brought bagels."

I snagged his elbow and dragged him inside. "I have an idea."

Noah ignored me and walked into the kitchen. He opened a drawer and pulled out a large knife, slid out a cutting board, and began to cut the bagels lengthwise.

"A lesbian couple —"

He stopped cutting. "No lesbians."

"One of them is cheating with another girl."

"You know I love lesbians just as much as the next guy. Remember what happened the time we tried to out Myrtle? They went ballistic. We almost lost our jobs."

"They can't fire us over a story line."

"They can do whatever they want. They're like

the mob. Just last week I saw another staff writer's picture on a milk carton in Von's. We can't do it. Lee won't go for it; the sponsors won't go for it; and I'm too good lookin' to die."

"It's provocative. Just one episode?"

Photo credit: Yael Swerdelow

15

I'm convinced the television and film industries were developed to keep us from having to build more prisons. Imagine people who manipulate talent for a fee. I once had lunch with an executive at ICM who told me that if she didn't like the tone of a person's voice who was speaking on the phone, she would trash their project, and she didn't care if it was *Gone with the Wind* she was squashing.

Lee Bender was no different. She was one of our producers at Movicide, the studio that put Heavy Myrtle on the air every week. Lee was a beautiful blond sweetheart who'd make any old-fashioned parent proud. She had scruples to the ceiling but no higher. She didn't need morals bigger than her office, because she hardly got the chance to use the ones she had.

Lee sat in her office petting the hair on the purple troll attached to her key chain like it was her favorite childhood doll. "I talked to the producers yesterday. They talked to our sponsors. They weren't thrilled. But they got back to us today and strangely enough, they approved it. Personally, I think it's a great idea. Lesbians are hot right now. I don't know how long it will last, but I love it. I love k. d. lang. I love Melissa. There is one thing we need to change. The affair has to be with a man, and the woman has to leave her lover for this man. That'll take care of the male demographic. Besides that, we love it."

"No!" I protested. "This is not about men. And this woman would never leave her true love for some passing thing with a lover, whom she'd only started seeing to avoid intimacy. She's afraid of getting hurt, so she's 'acting out' with this affair!"

Lee and Noah stared at me in disbelief. They always thought I was a loose cannon, but I knew these industry politics too well and it sickened me. I'd rather quit than become a hired gun for the creative equivalent of murderers.

Lee finally released her troll and keys, setting them on the table between us. I snatched up her troll and, unconsciously or not, begin twisting it's coarse, long purple hair.

Lee's eyes were glued to the troll. "I'm sorry. That's the best I can do."

"Well, that's not good enough," I argued.

“Well, let’s think about this.” Noah, sensing the seriousness of the situation, tried to smooth things out. “We can work with this, or we can do something completely different.”

“No, I’m tired of placating this patriarchal society. How are we going to create change if we don’t demand it?!” I pushed myself from the table and stood. “You know what? I quit!”

I slammed the troll onto the table. Lee rescued it immediately, stroking it into a frenzy.

Noah jumped up and put his arm around me. “She doesn’t mean that.” He looked at me deeply. “You don’t mean that.”

“Loretta, I understand your anger, but all we can really do is slowly chip away at the tyranny. You’re in a great position to do that. Besides, you’re under contract.” Lee glared at me like a bottom fish.

All I could see was red — and that damned purple troll.

16

I stormed out to the parking lot of Movicide; Noah followed a close second. I knew Lee and the big execs would never respond to reason, so I decided to play their way, through pure irrationality.

"Look, Noah, either you get that troll or I quit."

"Loretta, this is not 'I love Lucy.' " He put his hands on my shoulders and squeezed them together firmly. "You can't just go around stealing trolls from business executives."

"Just get the troll." I walked off towards my car.

17

A new banner hung behind the bar boasting SCORPIO PARTY with huge dayglow green scorpions that actually looked more like lobsters painted at each end of the sign. The place was littered with astrological paraphernalia. Blue glittering foam stars hung around the perimeter of the bar. Dozens of glow-in-the-dark moons and constellations shone from the usually darkened walls. And to create the quintessential celestial experience, a giant mobile of the planets in the solar system swung precariously from the dance floor ceiling. The Earth's stand-in, a huge disco ball, flickered psychedelic colors across the whole club. Music boomed from the deejay booth while Celia washed glasses and Kimba flirted with some customers.

Veronica and Tracy had become inseparable, and this night was no exception. Rachel and I were with them in the poolroom, playing doubles and losing miserably. Theoretically, we stood a chance at beating Tracy because Veronica was just learning. But it seemed as though Tracy enjoyed the handicap.

"Ya see, there's a trick to this shot." Tracy stood with her cue extended, pointing to the eight ball she intended to shoot in the side pocket. Three striped balls were between the cue and the eight ball. She had to jump the cue ball a foot and knock the eight in the pocket without the cue ball following it in there. "You've got to keep the stick aimed downward toward the table and at the same time try not to tear up the felt as you make the shot." Tracy shot the cue ball, which careened through the air sending the eight ball into the pocket to win the game.

I shook my head in disbelief. "Great shot, Trace."

Rachel, still in shock, stared at the felt. "I don't believe you made that shot!"

"We're such a great team, and I can't even play." Veronica jumped up and down while remaining in one place.

"Oh, sure you can. You just need to learn to whack 'em hard, and you'll get a ball in." Tracy gave Veronica a rub on the back.

Annie and Sandy entered the club wearing identical outfits; blue jean shorts, tank tops, and tennis shoes. They had either come together or were meant for each other. As they were also holding hands I assumed it was the latter scenario.

"I don't fuckin' believe it," I thought. At least I thought I had said it to myself.

"Oh, nice. What the fuck is that about?" fumed Rachel.

I didn't really hear Rachel. I was floored by the sight of Annie. She looked rejuvenated and healthier — if that were possible for a cyclist who would often ride from the valley to the beach, play a volleyball tournament, and ride home for a shower and night out on the town.

A few sentences out of Annie's mouth and this heart should beat regular. I had to talk with her. "Rache, I'm gonna go talk to Annie for a second; do you mind?"

"Yeah, I mind. What do you have to say to her?"

"I just haven't seen her in a while, and we left it on kind of a bad note. Ya know?"

"That's cool, 'cause I have to talk to Sandy," Rachel retaliated.

"What is this shit? Just because I'm gonna talk to Annie you have to make me jealous?"

"I'm not trying to make you jealous; I want to say hi to Sandy."

"Okay, forget it," I said. "I'm not gonna talk to Annie."

"Fine, I'm still gonna talk to Sandy."

"Fuckin' great."

Rachel walked away leaving me to stew in my own juices until I'd made jam. She stood at the Virgo table with Annie and Sandy. I decided to join them since we had all been so intimate anyway.

"Hey, you guys, how ya doing?" I said, sheepishly.

"Come on, Loretta, give me a hug," Annie said, warmly opening her arms. I could feel Rachel's eyes drilling a hole in my back, but I knew I had to hug her or it would have looked like I was trying to hide something. And I was.

"No hard feelings, huh?" offered Annie.

"No, not at all." I had to risk pissing Rachel off for my own sanity. "Can I talk to you alone for a minute?" I asked Annie.

"Sure, let's get a drink."

Annie turned to Rachel and Sandy who were now seated and chatting eagerly. "We're gonna get a drink; do you two want anything?"

"Just you," Sandy grinned dopily, looking much like a sheepdog.

"Well, you have that. How 'bout you, Rachel?"

"No, thanks," Rachel replied curtly and turned back to speak with Sandy. Cattiness was a new look for Rachel, and not a good one.

We walked over to the bar. Annie took the initiative and ordered drinks. "Two sex-on-the-beach, please."

Celia, who knew the story, rolled her eyes.

Annie insisted on paying, but backed down when I told her I never let girls buy me drinks because it always made me feel obligated to sleep with them. It wasn't the response I'd hoped for but we moved on. Celia set down two fruity beach drinks and I paid for them. Celia scowled at my intentions. She was way ahead of me.

Annie noticed the Scorpio theme and didn't quite know what to make of it. "So, are you a Scorpio, Loretta?"

"Sure am," I said confidently. Scorpios may have a reputation for being scary and evil, but there are few who've had better sex than with a Scorpio, and they'll nod knowingly when you admit to being one.

"They say Scorpios are really aggressive." Annie grabbed a bar stool and sat down while I stood next to her.

"Yeah, but I'm always stingin' myself in the back of the head."

A fellow scorpion overheard our conversation and swooped in. "I'm a Scorp," she said proudly. It was as if she'd been waiting all night for the Scorpio sexual festivities to begin and all she had to do was mention her Scorpio affiliation to get serviced. We looked at her blankly, and she shrugged and slithered away.

"So, you're with Sandy, huh? What a trip. I guess we switched partners."

"Yeah, isn't that so cosmic? I left Chauncey right after you and I broke it off." She looked at me intensely. "I think you gave me the courage to leave her. Then Sandy and I went out and really hit it off."

"That's great." I forced a smile. "Rachel and I are really happy, too."

"She's very pretty. She seems nice, too."

Was Annie one of those women who exuded sexuality with everyone, or did she still have feelings for me? I couldn't tell. "You know, I have to tell you, I had a junior heart attack when I saw you walk in just now."

"Really?" she said curiously.

"Yeah. I'm still really attracted to you . . ." I waited for a reaction and hoped for the right one, "you know?"

"Yeah? Well, I think you're attractive." Either she was completely stupid or she was letting me off the hook brilliantly. "I'll always miss your lips," she said flippantly.

"I guess that would be the difference between us. You'll always miss my lips, and I'll always miss you." I had my answer, but for some odd reason I chose to wallow.

"Well, I think we had a lot of fun together. I miss your smile, too, but I think it's all for the best. You're in love with Rachel, and Sandy and I are getting married."

"Really?" I said, glad my drink was on the bar and not in my mouth. "Wow, you guys?"

As soon as I heard the word *marriage* I felt inferior to her. Like my love for Rachel was a lie. Their love must be real; they're getting married.

"Well, that's great. So . . ." I glanced over toward Sandy and Rachel having the connection I had wanted. "They look like they're having a good time."

"Yeah, Sandy's so fun to be with," Annie said nonchalantly.

"I guess," I muttered.

We walked back to Virgo territory.

"So, you guys seem to be pretty cozy," I said aloud to Sandy and Rachel, when I really meant to think it lamely.

"Cozy? Oh, I forgot. Loretta gets jealous whenever the moon is full."

"Well, once a month seems healthy to me," Sandy offered generously.

Annie wrapped her arms around Sandy, pulling her in for a kiss.

"I love you," Annie said admiringly.

"I love you," answered Sandy.

They shared a moment, leaving Rachel and me in the dust.

"Well, we're gonna leave you two alone. Nice seeing you guys."

"Yeah, you guys make a great couple," volunteered Annie.

"Thanks," Rachel winced, as she bolted off for the libation station.

I followed her to the bar. "What was that supposed to mean, we're a great couple."

"Jesus, Loretta, are you fuckin' paranoid? She meant we were a great couple. Do you have a thing for her or what?"

"No, I dumped her, remember?"

"I remember you didn't have much choice. And what was the shit about me and Sandy being cozy? Sounds like you're projecting your guilt onto me."

"I have no guilt. And for your information, Annie was coming on to me."

Just as I finished using a lie to justify a cheat, in walks karma, in the form of J.R.

"Well, since she's so hung up on you, why don't you just go back with her?" asked Rachel angrily.

"Because I love you," I replied, matching tones.

"You coulda fooled me!" Rachel swung around

back to the bar, immediately encountering J.R., who had managed to eavesdrop a choice bit of the fight.

"Hey, babe! What's shakin'?" Rachel turned instantly sweet, giving J.R. a playful sock in the arm.

I looked away, disgusted with myself, our public display, and the Scorpio theme night.

"What's with her?" J.R. said loud enough for me to hear.

"The moon." Rachel hit J.R. again. "Let's get a drink." Rachel motioned for Celia.

I took refuge in the poolroom.

"Whad'ya do now?" Tracy said, smacking her gum and tapping her pool stick on the floor.

"Why do you think I did it?"

" 'Cause I heard your tail thumping when your ex walked in. Ya made her jealous, didn't ya?" Tracy looked at me sternly. "Mistake number one in the dyke drama hand guide, Loretta: Do not burn your hand carrying a torch for the ex."

"I can't believe she likes Johnnie-law-dog over there."

"Well, maybe she's just tryin' to get back at you," suggested Tracy.

I kept my eye on Rachel as J.R. picked up a lock of her hair and smelled it, then flipped it around, and petted it lovingly.

"Did you see that? She's touching her hair."

Veronica tried to soothe me. "Calm down, Loretta. You know Rachel's not interested in her. She loves you."

"Look, she's fuckin' strokin' her hair!" I exploded. "I don't believe this! I could kick her fuckin' ass!" I lunged for the bar, but Tracy clipped me by my collar and rubbed my shoulders like a prize fighter's corner man.

Veronica latched hold of my hand, massaging my palm aggressively. "Loretta, jealousy is a completely manmade emotion. It serves no purpose. Our control over our emotions is the only thing that separates us from animals."

I yanked myself free from both of them. "I thought it was our opposable thumb."

I tore off to the bar and wedged myself between Rachel and J.R. "Hey!" I said for lack of anything better coming to mind.

"Excuse me, we were having a private conversation." Rachel reacted to me as though I was just another bar hag.

"Yeah, I saw." I turned my sights to J.R. "Look J.R., I don't care if you are studying to be a Nazi, if you touch Rachel's hair one more time, I'm gonna hit you so hard the bar will feel it."

"Well, that's quite a threat, Loretta."

"It's a promise," I said.

"Cool it, you guys," Rachel said as she tried to move between us. "Let's get a drink or something."

"Rachel, stay out of this!"

Rachel took my hint and headed for cover by Tracy.

"Sounds like you're a little insecure about your girlfriend," provoked J.R.

"Yeah, well, I don't let my goldfish swim with piranhas, either!" I said as I poked her right in her sternum.

"Nobody ever pokes me!" She shoved me into the bar.

"Yeah, well I just did." I grabbed a drink and flung the liquid in J.R.'s face. She jumped me, entangling us in a catfight that I could only see from an aerial view. My eyes rolled back in my head and I could hear the sound of teeth gnashing, our fists flailing, occasionally connecting against flesh, but mostly against air. Celia gave Kimba the high sign, sending Kimba leaping over the bar like a pole vaulter. I must have been at a disadvantage, 'cause Kimba was pulling J.R. off me. Tracy came from behind and clamped me in a half nelson quicker than I could say uncle. We put up more of a struggle trying to get back at each other than during the initial fight.

"You guys are eighty-sixed! Outta here!" Kimba yelled as she did a backward rumba with J.R.

I shook Tracy off of me. "You can't eighty-six me!"

"I sure can — I can eighty-six my mother." Kimba dragged J.R. to the front door and shoved her towards it. "You're both out of here for the night!"

"You'll regret this, Loretta!" J.R. bellowed as she headed out the door. I fast walked after her like a rooster on speed. "Oh, yeah?" I yelled. "What are you gonna do, write me a ticket?!" Luckily she was out the door and didn't hear me.

Rachel stomped toward me. "You're outta control. You're being a complete jerk!" She paused as if she was waiting for a response she wouldn't be satisfied with, but she never received it. "I'm outta here!"

"Yeah, well guess what? I ain't comin' home. You can sleep alone tonight!" I regretted it as soon as I'd said it.

"Oh, I don't think I'll be alone!" she volleyed, as she stormed out of the club.

"That's gotta hurt," Kimba said under her breath so the whole bar could hear. I knew Kimba could never throw me out because Celia was such a pal, but she had to make a show of it for the cop.

"Ah, fuck this." I sat down on a stool next to Celia.

"Go after her and apologize. You guys can work this out." Veronica, the voice of reason presented her view.

"I don't want to work this out. She can have Robocop!"

Celia, who had watched the whole fight from the sidelines, finally spoke. "Now, hon, you just sit down and have a drink with us. We probably just had too many Scorpios in one place, that's all. You can spend the night at my house, and everything will be fine by morning. Either that or you'll be too hung over to care."

"C's right, Lo," Tracy said, handing me her club soda. "You guys just need a day to sort things out. You probably just had a little too much to drink."

"Yeah, well, I feel like I haven't had enough." I signaled to Kimba behind the bar. "Give me a drink and make it a stiffy."

18

It was the first time I'd ever hung out with Celia outside of the bar. She was even more complex than I had imagined. Her tastes were highly eclectic, ranging from reading French literature to listening to Stevie Nicks albums to watching classic horror films. We were halfway through *Nosferatu* and a bag of Jiffy Pop when I decided to go home. Celia insisted I needed time to fully understand the dynamics of why Rachel and I were creating this drama, but all I knew was I missed her miserably.

All kinds of nasty thoughts were lumbering

around inside my head. She had left the bar right after J.R. Perhaps they decided to have a grudge fuck. Celia sloughed this idea off as pure paranoia, but there is no limit to the irrational thoughts a mind can have while watching vampires with bad teeth.

The sun was coming up as I started off toward home.

I pulled up to my house about as fast as I could without driving into the living room. J.R.'s Jeep was not only parked in my driving space, the engine was cold. I gave the tire a swift kick, only because I didn't have a knife handy. I tried to pretend my foot didn't ache from the impulsive contact with the steel belted gatorback. I unlocked the door quietly. Being a masochist at heart, I wanted to surprise them in an act of passion. As I walked in and melodramatically yet nonchalantly hung my coat on the wooden rack by the door, I could see J.R. passed out in my only armchair. Rachel was just coming out of the kitchen with a glass of water.

"Shit! You scared the shit out of me!" Rachel said almost spilling her water.

I tried to act cool while my heart was ripping through my chest. "What's up?"

"Nothing. Nothing's up. What's up with you?" Rachel stood by the kitchen with the water as if everything were normal.

"What the fuck is she doing here?" I pointed to J.R. and sat down on the couch.

J.R. was zoned out, completely pacified by alcohol. It was as if she was passed out, but her eyes remained open. She sat upright, and her head nodded occasionally to follow movement.

Rachel helped J.R. grip the glass of water. "She got really drunk, and she couldn't drive home."

I stood up and grabbed Rachel by the arms to steady her focus on me. "Look, I am not your husband, and I am not gonna take this kind of shit. I'll kick her ass." I kicked the chair J.R. was seated in revitalizing the pain from having kicked her tires. "I could really kick her ass now."

"Look, I'll tell J.R. to leave." Rachel leaned down to rouse J.R. I felt almost sorry for her. She reminded me of a big hound dog that had just been neutered; still groggy, eyes bloodshot, head swaying. I couldn't make her drive home looking so helpless.

"She does look pretty drunk," I conceded. "If I ask you a question, do you promise to answer me truthfully?"

Rachel crossed her arms. "Yes."

"Did you kiss her?"

"No."

"You answered pretty quickly."

"Well, I knew the answer."

"Then she can stay." I relaxed on the couch, folding my hands behind my head trying to be cool. "You know, it'll feel kind of good to have a cop in the house — you know, secure."

"Fuck you," Rachel said slicing through what little tolerance I had. I usually like it when someone says "fuck you" to me. It's passionate and honest and can be a turn on if mixed with a pinch of irony. This time it just pissed me off. I jumped up and followed Rachel as she headed for the bathroom.

"How can you do this to me? You're so screwed up, you know that?"

"Yeah, I'm so screwed up," she said mockingly as she began to stuff pertinent items into her purse.

"Why can't you apologize or something?"

"For what? What am I apologizing for?"

"You are such a spoiled bitch. You don't even care if you hurt me. You don't even see it!"

"Yeah, I'm such a spoiled bitch," she said. "You know, I don't want to be with you right now." She looked around the house for something but refused to make eye contact.

"Oh, great. So you're done dealing with it."

"Yeah, I'm too tired."

"Why can't you get angry at me, argue with me, scream at me or something?" I yelled trying to shake her.

"I don't want to right now. Haven't you ever not wanted to deal with something right when it happens?"

"No, I'm in therapy." I grabbed the glass of water from J.R.'s hands and went into the kitchen to get her a refill.

Rachel confronted me. "Look, either you leave or I leave."

"If I leave, is J.R. staying?"

"I don't know."

I handed J.R. the glass. "How 'bout if I sleep on the floor with J.R.?"

"No, I want you to leave," Rachel insisted

"Well, what do I get out of it if I leave?"

"I don't know," she said, growing progressively more agitated.

"So wait, lemme get this straight. I just drove all the way from Celia's at four in the morning, and I find you with another girl, and you want me to leave 'cause you're mad?"

"Yes."

"Why don't you leave?" I asked, trying to get it all straight in my head.

"Because I'm asking you to. I can't see you right now. I don't even want to be around you."

"You know what, in years past, in other relationships, I would have left. But now I figure, if all I'm gonna have left is myself, I wanna respect myself. I'm staying. You leave if you have to."

"Okay." Rachel began to walk around the room collecting her things.

I walked over to J.R., who was becoming slightly more coherent with every glass of water.

"J.R., you're welcome to spend the night," I said, not wanting her to leave with Rachel.

"Okay, thanks," J.R. muttered.

"You can sleep on the couch."

Through her haze J.R. discerned that Rachel was getting ready to leave. "I don't know. I think I should be going."

"I love you, Loretta," Rachel said, stalling at the opened front door.

"You sure have a funny way of showing it." I looked into her eyes trying to understand her.

Rachel started to close the door after her. "Don't go!" I cried, grabbing the door open.

"I just can't stay with you now." Tears skidded across the surface of her eyes. "I have to think about things." Rachel walked down the steps leaving me behind her.

I collapsed against the inside of the door. Rachel's imitation of Greta Garbo flashed up on the screen of my mind. Had we lifted this scene from every Garbo picture ending? "Don't go! Stay! All right, leave if you have to, but never come back if you walk out that door!" And then after they leave, "Don't go!"

Why do closed doors remind me of death? The cold paint of the door sucked up to my cheek; I heard my heart beat through the wood. Didn't she know that we could think each other's thoughts so that when she schemed I could sense it and when she hurt I could feel it? Don't go, don't go, my mind repeated, but her car engine noise was unmistakable. I could hear her Volkswagen from twenty miles away. She sped off as fast as a bug with a rusty floorboard could take her.

J.R. sipped her water like *Nosferatu* savoring blood. She was becoming more alive with every pint. I lay down on the couch face first and gripped a pillow tightly to my body. I was reminded of an ad I had seen in an airline magazine for a pillow the length of a human body. I thought it would be the perfect pillow to clutch when fresh from a breakup. They could call it the lonely pillow.

Tears streamed down my face in silence. I once heard our bodies were 98 percent fluid, so I knew if I cried long enough I'd disappear. I forgot about J.R. planted in my chair. All that was left in the world was a hole. It seemed as if I had wept through pain farther back than three past lives. I was stumbling in plague torn Europe when J.R. broke the spell.

"She's a great girl." J.R. had been sobering herself on my tears.

"What the fuck do you know about it?" I grumbled, my head buried in my lonely pillow.

"She really loves you." She sucked up more water.

"No thanks to you." I turned to her for effect.

"She's my ultimate dream girl. I'd give anything to have her."

"You are such an asshole, J.R. Don't you know how painful it is to love someone like I love Rachel and not know whether I'm gonna lose her? It fuckin' hurts. Sometimes I'm so afraid she's gonna leave, it feels like death is looming over me."

She shook her head slowly like a hypnosis casualty. "I know what you mean. I felt that way before my mother died."

"So why would you want to make me feel like that? Why are you going for Rachel when you know I love her?"

"I told you. She's my dream. I'm in love with her."

"How can you love her? You hardly know her."

"How long does love take?"

I sat up, clinging to the pillow. "But look, I'm asking you to stay away from her. Can't you just stay away from her?"

"Shouldn't you be asking her this?"

I paused, weighing the validity of her statement. "You're right. You're still an asshole, but you're a right asshole."

"You know, I think we're a lot alike."

"God, I hope not," I said as I headed for the refrigerator for a couple of beers. I realized I'd rather be locked up with an enemy than alone with my own misery. I popped open the beers and offered one to the beast. "That would mean I, too, was a gutless opportunistic parasite that preyed on the weak moments of other people's relationships."

She held the beer in one hand and water in the other. "We both want love, and we'll do anything to get it." She raised the beer. "Thanks," she said. Then she read the bottle. "Saint Pauli Girl."

"Ya never forget your first girl," I said, remembering St. Pauli Girl's first ad campaign.

"Ha, yeah, I'll never forget mine."

"Probably 'cause she was a marsupial."

J.R. surprised me by actually taking offense to the inference. She stood up quickly and with much more agility than I had thought her capable of at the time. "When are you gonna quit cappin' on me? Look, maybe I should go." She walked toward the door, and I could see for the first time her belt was undone and her jeans were unbuttoned. I assumed this had been for comfort rather than as a result of an interrupted sex fest. I could see her flat stomach creeping down to a neatly manicured, dark furry knoll, a view that was abruptly obstructed by three Levi's buttons. I had never before seen J.R. as sexy, just as I had never gotten a rise out of the devil. But suddenly this vulnerability leaking through her cracks forced me to see her clearly. Her body was sleek and toned, masculine yet curvy. She could probably make girls swoon as she swaggered up to their driver's side window and demanded to see their license. And though she wouldn't kill to wear a gown to the policemen's ball, I could see she'd be a knockout in a tight black dress. There is nothing more enviable than a versatile girl.

"Don't go," I said, starting to feel lonelier than a beetle in a box.

She stopped at the door, turned, and looked at me sympathetically. "Why not?"

"I don't want to be alone."

"Yeah . . ." She stood at the door, spacing out on her hanging belt buckle.

I grabbed my basketball, which was sitting conveniently by the coffee shrine. Noah and I like to shoot hoops when we get writer's block. Well, he shoots, I run around him like a midget trying to get a piece of the ball. "Think fast," I said, gunning the ball at her.

She intercepted the ball adroitly. "Shit, you almost spilled my beer."

She propped her beer neatly against my ficus plant and tossed the ball back and forth in her huge hands. A mischievous grin crossed her face. She swung open the front door and bounced the ball toward the sagging hoop that hung over the garage. She made a couple of hook shots, a layup, and a free throw. I was never one for jocks or any girl butchier than me, but I couldn't help feeling a tad titillated with her macho display.

"Nice shootin', Tex." I leaned up against the porch post and tried not to squint in the glare from the hazy sun.

J.R. bounced the ball between her legs as she

walked towards me. "Thanks. I was All-State in high school for two years." She tossed me the ball.

I tossed it back. "Go to college?"

"I screwed up my knee." She bounced the ball and threw me a pass.

I caught it and spun it slowly in my hands. "That's gotta hurt. Why'd ya wanna be a cop?"

"I hate criminals."

"Yeah, well, I hate fire, but you wouldn't catch me runnin' through a blazin' one tryin' to put it out."

"Why do you hate cops?"

" 'Cause cops enforce the white male power system." I feigned tossing the ball towards her aggressively. She reacted quickly, but I had faked her out. I put the ball under my arm and brought it inside the house. I set it down.

She came in from behind me and shut the door. "Not all cops are white males," she said sternly.

"You don't think you're a white male? Last night you sure fought like a white male." I leaned against the hallway door.

"Look who's talking." J.R. pressed against the opposite doorjamb as if we were preparing for an earthquake. Just as our eyes met, she grabbed my shoulders and shoved me into the hallway, slamming me against the wall. She put a full court press on my body and found my mouth even as I tried to avoid hers. She stuck her tongue so far down my throat, my toes wiggled. She tore open my shirt sending buttons flying. One hand washed across my breasts as the other gripped me between my legs making me cream instantaneously. A flash of insecurity hit me, and I pushed her solidly across the hallway, smashing her to the opposing wall. She looked at me with this, yeah-now-what-are-you-gonna-do look. I didn't know what to do. I was burning for her, but this was all wrong. Wrong for whom? It felt great. I sucked her lips, practically biting them off. She backed me down the hall, throwing me onto the bed. She started to pull open my pants.

"I don't fuckin' believe this," I said, partially wanting to stop her. "This is not happening."

She opened my bra latch and kissed my breasts.

"Whoa, whoa, hold on." I pushed her off of me.

"What, what's wrong?" She looked up at me completely miffed.

"I hate you."

She smiled. "Yeah?" She bit my neck just above my collarbone shooting a frosty chill zigzagging through me. "You hate me?"

"Yes," I said, trying to regain my strength.

She bit me again, harder, looking for blood. "You hate me now?"

I could hardly speak. My neurons were firing sparks to my cunt. "Yes."

J.R. lifted me from the bed and eased me to the floor. She lay on top of me with her left leg pressed strategically against my pubic bone. "Yes?"

I clutched her shoulders and forced her up and off me. "Yes, I fuckin' hate you!" I ripped open her shirt and yanked her back on top of me. She dug her teeth into my neck, my shoulders. She ran them down my arms. She flung me over onto my stomach and nipped at my back like a hungry animal. Each bite was so deep, painful, and exciting I had to scream. She laughed at me and scraped her teeth down my spine sending shivers to every nerve ending.

She pulled my pants off as she sucked and gnawed at every inch of my back. Her hand reached up and slipped between my panties. She shoved her finger inside my wetness as she got on my back, gyrating her body against mine. Her mouth latched onto my neck holding me locked in place as she plunged another long finger inside me. She whispered in my ear, "I own you." I came immediately. I was soaked in a mixture of hatred and euphoria.

We fucked for hours in a frenzy of guerilla sex. It was a sweat-filled battle of will and power which we had both won and lost a dozen times over. Each time one of us would come the other would break out with a ritualistic laughter of triumph. It was lucky for us she hadn't yet been awarded a firearm, or we'd have both been killed.

19

It was midafternoon, which is never a good time to be in a bar unless you're there to pick up a paycheck or some good advice. I was hoping for good advice. Celia and Kimba were poised behind the bar scrubbing the rims of V-8 and Coke containers, conducting a sort of bar spring cleaning. I sat watching them for a while before I got up the nerve to speak.

"Do you guys love me unconditionally, no matter what I do?" I asked Celia and Kimba.

They both looked up from their respective tasks. "Whad'ya do?" Celia asked.

"I got it on with J.R."

There was a temporary silence while they stared at me. A combination of disbelief and horror swept the color from their faces.

"No fuckin' way!" Kimba said angrily.

"Yeah, way," I assured them.

"She's your nemesis," Celia kindly offered.

"Yeah, well, it just happened."

Celia took a step back from the bar. "Right. It was dark, and you bumped up against one another naked."

"She seduced me," I insisted.

Celia reached out her hand, gently grasping my own. "Does Rachel know?"

"No, I haven't talked to her yet. I don't wanna tell her. She'll leave me in a hot flash."

"Well, babe, you're gonna have to tell her."

She gave my hands a little shake for emphasis.

Kimba leaned across the bar with an air of finality. "Don't tell her," she said firmly.

"If you don't tell her, Miss Dragnet will," Celia argued, unraveling Kimba's stance without even looking at her.

"Don't tell her," Kimba reiterated.

Celia squeezed my hand tightly. "J.R. wants Rachel like a bear wants a nap. She'll do anything to break you two up."

"It seemed like she really liked me," I said meekly.

They glanced at each other knowingly, then at me. They thought I was naive. Maybe I was. I wanted desperately to be relieved of my guilt, while still being allowed to wallow in the memory of the morning's incredible sexual escapades. I could smell J.R.'s scent wafting up from my palms. How could something smell so edible and vile at the same time.

20

Tracy was always working on her '52 baby blue Chevy pickup. I didn't even think there was anything wrong with that truck. But there she was, day after day, sprawled out on her slide board under the engine, bathing herself in oil and grease. I would tease her and say she just liked to lie beneath anything that was raised on blocks.

Tracy lived in a garage converted loft surrounded by a huge dirt yard lined with storage units. Not the ideal place to raise a child, but all Tracy had was a goose.

Since the feedback from my bartender buddies had been mixed, I thought I'd run my J.R. incident past Tracy and Veronica. Veronica stood patiently by Tracy's side. Occasionally, Tracy would slide her dolly out from under the monster vehicle so Veronica could hand her a tool. They had an odd symbiotic relationship which was a little too benign for my tastes.

I related my predicament to them with as few details as possible while still maintaining the flavor of the heated event. Tracy had listened to most of the story while fully visible to us on her dolly, but upon hearing the ending she seemed disgusted and quickly disappeared under the truck.

I got down on my knees, bent below the shiny chrome bumper, and looked for her. "Trace, at least say something."

She gripped the bumper with both hands and slid herself out. "You know, I used to consider you one of the most scrupulous people I knew." Tracy tried to wipe the sweat off her face only managing to smear herself with grease war paint instead. "Believe it or not, Loretta, I looked up to you when I wasn't feeling sorry for you."

"Thanks." I rose to my feet. I didn't need to take her abuse on my knees.

"But this is completely wrong," Tracy added, trying to gain back my attention.

"Wrong? That sounds distinctly like a value judgment to me."

"Loretta, I'm not your therapist, I'm your friend. I can make value judgments. I think it's wrong, and I don't want to hear about it anymore." Tracy flung herself back under her truck.

Veronica, who had been smirking self-assuredly throughout our conversation, piped up. "Loretta, if you're stupid enough to violate your fidelity, you have to be smart enough not to be honest about your stupidity."

"What?" I said, trying to grasp the inner meaning of what she'd expressed.

Tracy reappeared to clarify her stance. "You know, Loretta, there are some things we just don't do in the South, and fuckin' our enemies is one of 'em."

21

Friends never tell you what you want to hear. You have to have a dog for that. I sat by the pool with Noah, watching him slather his chest with suntan lotion. Nice chest for a guy, I thought. Noah enjoyed my tale of lust and deceit much more than everyone else. His judgment was clear and simple. "You guys shouldn't have moved in together. Living with someone has a terrible misery/bliss ratio. I prefer being totally alone rather than feeling lonely in a relationship."

"You're twisted."

"Yeah," he agreed as he raised his hand revealing something he'd been hiding. "But I got the troll." The troll glistened in the sunlight. He, too, was covered in suntan oil.

22

I did not seriously think the troll could be used as leverage to persuade Lee Bender to use my lesbian story line in a Heavy Myrtle episode. How much leverage can one derive from a three-inch tall purple-haired troll, even when used as a fulcrum?

However, the troll did possess great potential to stimulate creativity and nonsense, the tools of trade for any cartoon writer.

Noah and I dressed up like fashion victims from bad film noir. He was in his black trenchcoat, layering his double-breasted baggy suit with a silver flask of bourbon. I was in my veiled hat and driving coat, waving a gold cigarette holder like I was dying for someone to light me up.

We drove to the depths of downtown L.A. for the sound and feel of hostage situation realism. We huddled together in one of the few working phone booths in the area and phoned our producer. I deposited a quarter in the slot — as the phone company knew well, dimes never traveled in pairs.

"Lee Bender's office," a distinguished male assistant answered.

I sheepishly pushed the phone receiver in Noah's face.

Thinking quickly, he said, "Yes, George Hamilton for Lee Bender, please."

I shot him a look of surprise at his celebrity name choice. I nuzzled up to him and listened into the receiver.

"This is Lee Bender," her confused voice uttered.

Noah placed his handkerchief over the mouthpiece to further muffle his disguised voice. "We're holding your troll hostage," Noah said in a Bogiesque tone. He pulled the troll from his coat pocket and placed it on top of the telephone booth for effect. A rubber band had been cleverly crisscrossed and bound the troll's hands and feet, making a clean getaway impossible.

We could hear the sound of panic and jingling keys across the line as Lee was thrown into a panic.

"Who is this? How did you get my troll?" Her voice trembled.

"Never mind that. We have him," Noah answered

emphatically. "He hasn't eaten in hours, and he's lookin' a little haggard." We looked at the troll, his hair matted, eyes glazed over.

We both began to laugh uncontrollably. Noah pushed the phone my way.

I tried imitating a Dead End Kid. "Here are our demands," I said hoarsely. "One of Myrtle's lesbian clients is having an affair with a male rookie cop, but she returns to her lesbian lover in the end. Work it out or you'll never see your troll again." I hung up the receiver.

Noah tipped his fedora downward hiding his face. I considered hailing a cab, but that would have been silly. We had my car. I dropped Noah off at home. We decided he was to keep the troll because I had no tolerance for torture.

23

I had plenty of time to think while I drove down the Ventura freeway during rush hour. The buildings bordering the freeway moved faster than the cars.

I had spent the whole day reveling in my ability to transform intense hatred into an act of love via sex with J.R. Suddenly, for the first time that day, I was overwhelmed with feelings of pain and guilt. I had been unfaithful to Rachel, the woman I loved more than anyone on the planet. But it wasn't the fact of having sex with someone else that made me feel bad. I'd had an incredible experience without her.

She would not understand. I knew the most damaging part of infidelity is the dishonesty. Every new experience two people withhold from each other causes them to grow farther apart until they no longer know each other.

I would never want Rachel to feel pain over something so insignificant as my ego problems. J.R. had me so frightened and threatened that I jumped through her hoop like a common circus mouse. I ached inside for what I had done. I sat in my car, surrounded by thousands of other vehicles in a commuters' graveyard. I wondered if anyone had ever died from guilt. What is guilt really though? It's not really an emotion. It is more like a catalyst that triggers emotions. It sits as idly as dynamite until the fuse is lit. I was lit and ready to explode. I was certain at that moment that the curious phenomenon called *spontaneous combustion* was really just an overdose of guilt. The highway patrol would find my abandoned car in the fast lane with hardly a trace of me, just a small pile of ash and the distinct odor of matzo ball soup.

When I finally reached my street, I almost drove past my own house. There in the driveway sat J.R.'s bright red Jeep, the omen of imminent heartache. I hopped out of my car to see J.R. walking out of my house carrying a box filled with Rachel's stuff. No wonder she was a cop. She'd have been a failure as a thief, robbing our house in broad daylight. She was dressed up like the CHP poster girl, clad in her LAPD shirt, her America's Most Wanted hat, and black secret service-style sunglasses. All she needed was a mustache. She set the box down in the back of her Jeep, leaned against her gigantic off-road tires, and flashed a scowl of a smile.

"What, are you moving in?" I said off-handedly, feeling the warm shawl of sarcasm wrap around my emotions.

"No, I guess Rachel's moving out." She stood motionless, arms crossed in bully fashion, like I hadn't seen the sweet face she makes when she comes.

"And you work for U-Haul?" I pushed past her and walked toward the house. The door was open. Rachel was kneeling on the floor sorting through our collective CD's. Why must CD's always bear the brunt of every breakup? We buy music together in harmony, then divide it callously. I stood watching Rachel having a moment of fond reminiscence while reading the lyrics of k.d. lang's "Ingenue" CD. We'd purchased it together. She grinned fondly and placed it generously in my pile.

J.R. stepped in behind me, drawing Rachel's attention toward me. Rachel almost smiled. It was too sad to be a smile, too tender for a funeral.

"You want me to leave?" J.R. said, presenting a smooth imitation of sensitivity.

"No, stay." Rachel stood up slowly. "We have nothing to hide."

"J.R., please leave, or I'll have to call the cops."

"Look, maybe I should wait outside." J.R. motioned for the door without moving, a neat trick if you can pull it off.

"I want you to stay," Rachel reiterated.

"She doesn't need to see this." I wanted to erase J.R. like a bad character in Heavy Myrtle.

"Apparently she saw everything already."

The worst case scenario was materializing before me. "Rachel," I said, "it's not what you think."

"From what I heard, she was drunk, and you seduced her."

"Seduced her? Please, I still have the barrel marks where she held the gun to my back."

"That's a good one," J.R. said under her breath while walking to sit on the couch. What was she going to do? Watch us like we were her favorite sitcom?

"Don't you have some children to accost?" I exclaimed fiercely.

"Leave her alone," Rachel defended her. "This is not her fault."

"Whose fault is it?" I said. Open mouth, insert foot.

"I told you never to cheat on me. I told you I would leave you."

"You know something? I've been in long-term relationships before, unlike you and Kojak over here, who has probably been through more women than a speculum. I know what it's like to be cheated on, and, honey, this was not it."

"What was it then?" Rachel waited patiently for my answer.

"It was a mistake." I stood my ground knowing I had none.

"A mistake! Ha! I suppose you're gonna tell me that you'll never do it again?"

She had been avoiding my eyes, fearing they'd weaken her. I grabbed her arms, forcing her to look at me squarely. "No, I won't tell you that I'll never again for the rest of my life sleep with anyone else.

We're gonna have a long life together, and I can't write insurance policies. But I can tell you that I'll love you, and I'll be honest with you."

She tore herself away from me. "You are pathetic! Why the fuck would I commit to you if you're not going to be monogamous?"

"No one's monogamous! You think Troglodyte over here —"

"Troglodyte?" J.R. interrupted, either offended by the word or excited to hear about cave dwellers.

"— isn't gonna cheat on you? She'll just lie through her prehistoric teeth that she's being faithful."

"Hey . . . wait a minute," J.R. said, this time obviously offended.

"You want to know why I slept with J.R.? I'll tell you why I slept with J.R." A cruel silence fell across the room. Rachel and J.R. looked at each other, then back at me, both anxious to hear my next words. Rachel sat on the couch next to J.R., giving me her full attention. I wasn't sure what words I was about to say, but I knew they would have to come out in sentences.

"It's hard to believe, but I think I hated her so much that it turned me on." Again they looked at each other, mocking me. How did J.R. get to go home from school early while I was being held after and punished? She did it, too, I wanted to say. But I didn't. I plowed onward, becoming more and more animated as I spoke.

"We were sitting around just hating each other in a healthy way, and I felt close to her, and I thought, I can't do this, this isn't right. But then I thought to myself, when I'm ninety years old and suckin' my dinner through a straw, I'm gonna look back on my life — not your life or her life but my life — and I want to feel that I have lived the way I wanted to, with unbelievable highs and devastating lows and even mistakes. And I won't regret doing what I needed to do for myself."

Rachel and J.R. sat perfectly still for a moment. I didn't expect applause, nor did I expect what followed.

Rachel rose to her feet and put her face aggressively close to mine. "If you think in some Bohemian fantasy of yours that shit's gonna fly with me, you are so wrong." She earned a pause. "No matter how you try to justify it, you cheated on me, and I can't forgive that." She knelt down and began tossing her CDs into a box.

"Honey, there are a lot of more important things to worry about in a relationship than infidelity."

She stopped momentarily. "Yeah, like what?"

"You're using J.R. You don't even like her." I could feel J.R. shrink with embarrassment, but I didn't care. She should have left when she had the chance. "You're just scared to death of getting close to someone. You're scared of loving me as much as you do." I had struck a nerve, while hoping more for an artery.

"I want you to leave now." Rachel stood up and stared right through me.

"Honey, this is bullshit. We don't have to do this. We can love each other." I moved toward her to hold her, kiss her, anything.

She pushed me away. "Just go. Just get the fuck out of here. Just go!" She flung her hands in the air, which was thick with the presence of J.R.

J.R. sat uncomfortably watching something she had no comprehension of, nor any right to be witness to, but she had missed her exit cue so she tried to remain unobtrusive.

"Honey?" I tried to reason with Rachel through the mere inflection of my voice.

"Just go, will you? Get the fuck outta here! Just fuckin' leave!" Rachel yelled louder.

"Please don't do this. We don't have to do this." I tried to forget about J.R. and to calm Rachel down so we could speak rationally.

"Then I'll fuckin' leave," Rachel said, bolting down the hallway toward the bedroom. She immediately came stomping back with her car keys in hand, threw open the front door, stormed out, slammed the door behind her.

I stood there in shock, numb but breathing. J.R. stood up and approached me. She reached out to put her arm around me, perhaps not knowing what else to do. I peeled away from her, wincing at the very thought of being touched by her again.

"Could you please go?"

She slowly withdrew and crept out the door.

24

Over the following weeks I stumbled through an ugly range of emotions. I'd fucked up. I knew the feeling. It was like my umbilical cord had just been cut and I was floating out there alone in the universe. The funny thing about being all alone is it's not funny at all. I was wandering from room to room as though Rachel would be there eventually. I wondered if there was such a thing as object permanence. Object permanence is a stage infants reach when they test reality to see if they can hide an object, like a toy duck, underneath a blanket, and the duck reappears when they remove the blanket. This can keep the average infant happily busy almost to adulthood. Before an infant reaches this stage, if you hide their duck, they think it never existed in their known universe. Mom leaves the room, the infant thinks, Mom who? Rachel left; sometimes I wonder if there ever was a Rachel.

I knew part of my delirium was due to the fact that I hadn't been eating right. Okay, I hadn't been eating. Mostly I just lay on my couch, doubled over, coughing up my heart. I talked to myself aloud a lot of the time and never had nice things to say. I didn't answer the phone whether it rang or not. There was no one I wanted to hear from except Rachel, and she was too strong willed to call me. She had quit chewing gum when she was seven and hadn't touched the stuff since.

I missed Rachel terribly.

Sometimes in the middle of the night I had been awakened by her arms wrapped tightly around me. She'd be kissing me with such force, then she'd say, "I love you so much." In the morning, she wouldn't remember a thing. She was a sleep kisser.

I loved Rachel so much it hurt, and yes, of course, I wanted it to hurt her, too. Solitary suffering is so much more painful. In fact, I wanted everyone on the planet to be experiencing the excruciating pain of their own private breakups.

I was glad I didn't know where Rachel was staying or I would have called her. Once, after a heavy breakup, I'd set a girl's number by the phone on a big note which read, DON'T EVER CALL HER. CALL ANYONE ELSE, BUT DON'T CALL THIS NUMBER, and then I wrote the number. But over time the note had bowed, and soon all I could read from the upright angle was, CALL THIS NUMBER and her phone number, so I called her obsessively.

It's hard to retain the drive to keep on living after a breakup with someone I truly loved. Lesbian laboratory rats had been repeatedly found to perish soon after their long-term partner had been removed from the cage. I couldn't let that happen to myself. I had to go on with my life. I didn't want to ever again feel like I could die if someone I loved left me. I had to love myself. Before I could love anyone else, I had to love myself.

25

A new sign hung over the bar. GET JUICED NATURALLY, FRESH JUICE BAR. Celia's new motif was obvious. The club resembled a farmers' market taking place in a wax museum. Celia had informed me that her initial use of fresh fruit and vegetables was not only costly, she had encountered a fruit fly problem that was disturbing the customers. Fancy carrot, squash and watermelon decorative lights dangled from the bar area while much more elaborate designs brightened the whole bar.

Each table had an oversize vegetable centerpiece

that not only lit up, it flashed at the rate consistent with that particular vegetable's imagined personality.

Three-tiered metal baskets hung sporadically throughout the pool area and dance floor filled with varied assortments of kale, celery, tomatoes, lettuce, cabbages, peaches, pears, plums, nectarines, and squash of all shapes and sizes. The bar was like a giant cornucopia spilling out onto Lankershim Boulevard.

I sat at the bar between four blenders filled with protein smoothies of every variety. Celia was now in direct competition with coffeehouses and juice bars all over the city. The bar was packed with a new and eclectic mix of younger, hipper, trendier lesbians with great teeth.

It was strange to be back in the club after such a long time. The bar had changed but Celia was the grounding force who always made me feel welcome.

"So how are you doin', babe?" Celia rested her head in her hands and leaned towards me. "Still crouched in the fetal position?"

"I just wonder when the pain will end." I took a sip of my banana-and-mango protein drink.

"It never ends. It just becomes old pain."

We both paused at the weight of that thought. Then Celia had another thought. Reaching behind the bar, she pulled out an old crank-style juicer. She attached it to her side of the bar and ducked down under the freezers, only to reappear with a large flat of sprouted wheat grass and some clipping shears. The wheat grass grew in thick, healthy strands with a vivid bright green coloring that would have made my pool man and gardener proud. Celia skillfully wielded her giant hedge-clipping shears and began snipping clumps of grass, which she'd stuff into her ancient juicer.

"What are you doing?" I asked, mesmerized by her newfound joy in food processing.

"I'm diversifying for the times." Celia placed a small cup under the juicer's spout and began the arduous process of twisting the crank. Eventually minute amounts of rich dark green liquid came trickling down the spout. It seemed like a lot of work for little glory.

"It looks like plant puke," I commented needlessly.

"It's wheat grass. Try it." She pushed the tiny cup forward.

I lifted the cup, remembering all the many favors Celia had done for me over the years. She had once helped me reprogram a girl who had a fatal attraction to me. The girl was convinced I was her true love after a only few hours of conversing with a group of us at the bar. She refused to hear my conflicting feelings on the matter. She would call the bar and come in every night scouting for me, ready to win me over at any cost, namely mine. She wasn't violent exactly. Suffice it to say she was incredibly strong and broke things unwittingly. Celia convinced the girl that Celia and I had been lovers for many years but kept it under wraps so the bar would not suffer any unnecessary loss of clientele.

I drank cautiously and made a face only appropriate for wheat grass consumption. It tasted as bitter as the word *chlorophyll* sounded. I nodded my head encouragingly to Celia, appreciating her effort.

Feeling an odd presence, I casually turned to notice J.R. sauntering up to the bar. She wore a cocky grin on her mug.

"Hey, J.R.," I said to her, not wanting her to know I'd been buried knee deep in grief since I'd last seen her. "What's happenin'?"

"I'm waiting for someone." She glanced towards the entrance.

"Someone else's woman no doubt," I said bittersweetly.

"Could be yours," she countered.

"I'll let you know if I recognize her." I turned back toward Celia, signaling her to pony up another shot of wheat grass. Suddenly the flavor had grown on me. "How could I ever have liked someone like her?" I asked Celia.

" 'Cause, babe," Celia once again slowly cranked me out a shot. "J.R. is the dark side of the force that we wish we could be."

"What are ya, a Jungian bartender?"

"No, I saw *Star Wars* three times."

We both laughed and drank some wheat grass. I spotted the hair on the back of Celia's neck become erect as Annie walked in the bar. She slinked directly over to J.R. in her lusty and aloof style. Her torn jeans no longer made my heart go pitter pat, so I falsely assumed I'd lost my heart.

"I should've known. It's Psycho Jock. Well, at least it wasn't Rachel," I confided in Celia.

"Rachel has more class than to fall for that thing," Celia said.

"Hey, watch it. I slept with that thing." We both stared at the two of them. I thought they could be the most perfectly sinister match yet.

J.R. and Annie kissed almost attractively, then turned and walked toward the bar to order a drink.

"Hi, Loretta, how are you?" Annie said smiling at me sincerely.

"I'm cool. How are you?"

"I'm fantastic!" she said, and I was sure she was lying.

"Yeah? So what are you doing with Miss Thing here?" I said, delicately tapping J.R. on her sternum. "Did you and Sandy split up?"

"No, we just decided we'd see other people for a few months before we get married." Only Annie could have said this so it sounded convincing.

"You didn't call me," I said, dash of sarcasm, trace of truth.

"I thought you were with Rachel," Annie merrily jabbed.

"Yeah, aren't you with Rachel?" J.R. jumped in, smelling fresh flesh.

I moved Annie aside and stood threateningly close to J.R. "What's it gonna take for me to get you off my back?"

"Turn over," she smirked.

"I've already tried that." I was getting taller by the second.

Kimba noticed the commotion. "Okay, okay, down, big girls."

Celia took over, releasing the tension with an offer. "Let's all have a drink on the house, like that's something new."

Celia, determined to calm her patrons with anything other than alcohol, shoved more wheat grass in the juicer. Annie noticed Celia's endeavor.

"Shots of wheat grass. What a great idea." Annie

flashed a sexy grin at Celia. It was a huge flirtation, and it didn't take an involuntarily celibate bartender to figure it out.

"Thanks," Celia said shyly. She poured the drinks and distributed them across the whole bar. Everyone picked up their juice and stared at it indifferently, except for Annie who was obviously no stranger to wheat or any other kind of grass.

Celia held up her glass and all followed. "A toast," she paused, grasping for courage, "to the bartender, who needs to get laid."

Everyone froze, perhaps in prayer, but more likely in shock, as Celia never revealed her own problems. She was always there for everyone else. We had never really considered she might want sex. The noise level dropped. Celia, feeling Kimba's eyes burning holes in her, looked down the bar.

Kimba was laughing, but she stopped as soon as she caught Celia's glance. She threw up her hands. "Hey, it could happen."

The girls resumed breathing and drank their juice with varying reactions to its bouquet.

Everyone suddenly turned toward the entrance. It was like a straight celebrity had dropped in for a pickup. I turned to see Rachel and Sandy standing at the door. They were too busy absorbing the new, low-concept health decor to notice that half the bar was expecting imminent warfare while the other half was weighing Rachel or Sandy's potential as a future partner. The night was abuzz with possibilities.

"Could this get any weirder?" I turned and asked Celia.

"Could it get any more predictable?" she responded glibly. "Step right up, ladies, the first one's on the house," she called out to our new guests as I tried not to shrink into oblivion.

As Rachel and Sandy approached the bar, I realized I did have a heart, and it didn't belong to Sandy. My heart was a big thumping thing, and if I'd had a tail it would have been wagging. Rachel looked renewed and angelic. I guess our breakup had been good for her; too good.

"Hey, babe, what's goin' on?" Rachel said smiling charmingly and swirling her hand around my yearning back.

"Well, I was just sittin' here minding my own business when my life started to flash before me," I said, hoping I wasn't too swollen and pale from all my indoor crying sessions.

"Can I talk to you alone?" Rachel said gently.

"Okay," I said.

Celia watched us approvingly as we walked to an empty artichoke table. We sat down. I don't mind sitting at tables.

"How are you?" Rachel asked, nervously placing her hand on top of mine.

"How am I?" I pulled away slowly for effect.

"I love you and I miss you. And I've been doing a lot of thinking about what happened," she started in.

I panicked about what I was about to hear and tried to change the subject. "Good. Me too. Where have you been staying?"

"I've been sleeping at Sandy's."

"Oh, lovely," I said jealously.

"We are just friends. I'm in love with you."

"Yeah? Well, you know what? I'm falling in love with me, too. I don't know if I can see both of us at the same time," I said, sorry I'd said it.

We heard some commotion over by the bar that drew our attention. Sandy and J.R. were getting into a scuffle over Annie and were working their way through the bar towards the pool table. Just another bar fight.

Rachel resumed speaking. "Do you mean that?"

"Not really."

We were again interrupted by the loud commotion at the pool table. Sandy and J.R. argued and pushed each other, disrupting Veronica and Tracy from their passionate embrace.

"She's mine!" Sandy yelled at J.R. while expertly pinning her to the top of the pool table by using a pool cue to secure her in place.

"I don't see any ring on her finger!" J.R. screamed back, in her uniquely arresting manner.

Celia, who had weak knees, signaled Kimba, the hired thug. Kimba leapt over the bar to break up the fight. Annie followed closely behind, basking in the glory of a fight held in her honor.

"What are ya gonna do now, huh?" Sandy taunted J.R.

Tracy and Kimba attempted to pry Sandy off of J.R., but she had her feet wedged in the pool table pockets.

"Let go, Sandy, or I'm gonna hafta hurt ya!" Tracy hollered.

Rachel and I went right back into our conversation.

"Actually, I feel pretty bad about what I did," I admitted. "I guess I was so busy ranting, I totally disregarded your feelings. I'm sorry for hurting you."

Rachel took my hands lovingly in hers. "You know, I think you did what you did because I was afraid to get really close to you, and maybe . . ." Rachel pointed to J.R., who had managed to get Sandy off of her and now had Sandy pinned against the pool table. Kimba was mangled in with them.

Tracy grabbed Sandy. "Let go of her J.R.!"

Veronica, who had been watching with hand-in-mouth horror up to this point, actually squealed, "No, no, no, no, no, no, no!" as she grabbed J.R. as firmly as she could and ripped her away from Sandy. J.R. shook Veronica off like water off a duck's back.

Rachel continued undaunted. "Maybe you slept with her because she let you get close."

Again we were interrupted as J.R. and Sandy began round two, skidding across the floor like a high school dance troupe.

"Well, she did have me right about where she's got Sandy right now," I said, referring to the way J.R. was trying to insert Sandy into the jukebox. We stopped talking and watched as Kimba and Tracy grabbed J.R. and threw her on the sofa.

"J.R., you are eighty-sixed!" Kimba said, having had enough live-action-hero fight scenes for one evening.

"She started it!" J.R. said, displaying her wonderfully advanced capacity for reasoning.

"You always start it," Kimba said, shaking J.R. by the shoulders. "Even when they start it, you really start it."

J.R. sprang to her feet, walked to the front entrance, and turned back to address the crowd. "I can't help it if you're all a bunch of jealous and insecure lesbians! I'll be back!"

"I know you will," Kimba said, returning to the

security of her station behind the bar and in front of the babes.

Veronica rushed to Tracy's side. "Are you all right?"

"Yeah, that was just a catfight." Tracy wrapped Veronica up in her big arms. "It's not like separating a couple of pit bulls. Now, that can scar ya." They collapsed onto the couch and launched into extreme PDA's (public displays of affection).

Sandy was just starting to suck up to Annie when Kimba noticed her. "You're outta here too, Sandy."

"Ah, this is bullshit!" Sandy started a junior tirade. "You saw her kiss Annie right in front of me."

"Annie has a brain?" Kimba said calmly.

"Yeah," Sandy retorted defiantly.

"You two are separated?" Kimba prodded.

"Well, kind of . . ." Sandy looked to Annie to bail her out. "Will you come with me?"

"No, I think I'm gonna stay," Annie said, turning back to Sandy. "Why don't you take Rachel, since she lives where you're going?"

Annie walked to the bar and settled her sights on Celia.

"I don't believe this shit," Sandy ranted as she shuffled over to us. "Hey, Rachel, do you want a ride home?"

"No, thanks. I think I'm gonna stay a while."

Sandy flung her hands in the air. "This place is so unhealthy!" She stormed out of the bar angrily.

Annie stared seductively at Celia, who was busy stuffing a carrot into a modern juicer.

"Celia," Annie said alluringly. "Let's make a toast to a bartender who needs to get laid."

Celia stopped what she was doing, gulped, and picked up a shot glass filled with green goo. "Yeah? Okay." Annie raised her glass, wrapping her arm suggestively around Celia's as they drank from each other's glass.

"It really could happen," Annie said, pulling back slowly from her sip without releasing her eyes from Celia's.

Kimba nodded with disbelief at Annie's interest in Celia.

Rachel and I stared at each other — the kind of stare which could only be attributed to love or unbridled lust.

"What are we doing here?" Rachel asked, standing up.

"We met here."

"That doesn't mean we have to live here," Rachel said, tucking my arm around hers.

"Yeah, you're right. It's so unhealthy," I said miming Sandy's words.

We stood and took a long glance around the bar. Tracy and Veronica were wrapped up like a pretty bow on a wedding gift, and I was sure their marriage was not far off. Tracy had always said she wanted another goose, but I really suspected she had transposed her maternal instincts onto geese, and would have been much more fulfilled with children. I voted Tracy and Veronica most likely to get married and have little ones. We blew the bar a good-bye kiss and strolled out into the night.

26

Rachel and I were curled up on the couch watching the end of the latest episode of the Heavy Myrtle show. We had invited Lee Bender and Noah over so we could have a sort of homecoming for the troll as we reunited it with its loving owner. Lee embraced her troll with a new sensitivity. She fixed its hair immediately, stroking the troll until I'm sure it was ready for another vacation by the pool. She thought it looked tanner, but we assured her it was just some residual oil.

On the TV screen we watched as Myrtle floated

in the air holding hands with two women wearing parachutes. One of the female cartoon characters looked conspicuously like Rachel; the other was a dead ringer for me. I had pulled a couple strings with the animator. I thought it would be a nice gift for Rachel to be immortalized as a cartoon. Heavy Mytrle's superhero flying ability kept these women airborne. All Myrtle had to do was hold them with her fleshy palms and they could fly too.

"I'm afraid of getting too close. I'm afraid if I do, I'll get left," said Libby, the character who possessed more than Rachel's physical attributes.

"How do you feel about what she's saying to you, Nina?" Heavy Myrtle inquired.

"I can relate. I'm afraid, too," said Nina, the cartoon girl who looked and acted like me, but seemed much more colorfully dressed than I'd ever been.

"You are?" Libby queried.

"Yes," Nina answered.

Myrtle glanced at the timer attached to her wrist. "Well, we have to stop now . . ." Myrtle said.

She then lets go of the girls' hands while pulling their parachute rip cords. The girls are suddenly yanked upward from the force of their chutes opening. Myrtle then punches her stopwatch clock at exactly fifty minutes. Several birds fly by Myrtle. She watches them glide by. "It doesn't matter if you're a seagull and a dove, a pelican and a crane, or two peregrine falcons. Love is love. It's all about the relationship. And just remember . . . if I can fly, you can fly." She spread her arms lovingly and began to fly off into the horizon.

Noah sat in my cushy chair, seemingly satisfied

with the story line of that show. Rachel gave me a warm kiss on the cheek. Lee, who was sitting comfortably next to us on the couch fondling her troll, had a huge smile on her face when the show ended.

"I just love that ending." Lee's eyes were aglow. "You know, we could even get a lesbian spin-off out of this episode."

"I think I have some material we could use," I said, making an incidental pitch.

"No lesbians," Noah pleaded.

Lee, Rachel, and I all snapped our heads toward him in unison. Noah winced slightly. We all turned back toward the TV and smiled as we watched the credits roll.

FOR LOVE AND FOR LIFE: INTIMATE PORTRAITS OF LESBIAN COUPLES by Susan Johnson. 224 pp. ISBN 1-56280-091-4 14.95

DEVOTION by Mindy Kaplan. 192 pp. See the movie — read the book! ISBN 1-56280-093-0 10.95

SOMEONE TO WATCH by Jaye Maiman. 272 pp. 4th Robin Miller Mystery. ISBN 1-56280-095-7 10.95

GREENER THAN GRASS by Jennifer Fulton. 208 pp. A young woman — a stranger in her bed. ISBN 1-56280-092-2 10.95

TRAVELS WITH DIANA HUNTER by Regine Sands. Erotic lesbian romp. Audio Book (2 cassettes) ISBN 1-56280-107-4 16.95

CABIN FEVER by Carol Schmidt. 256 pp. Sizzling suspense and passion. ISBN 1-56280-089-1 10.95

THERE WILL BE NO GOODBYES by Laura DeHart Young. 192 pp. Romantic love, strength, and friendship. ISBN 1-56280-103-1 10.95

FAULTLINE by Sheila Ortiz Taylor. 144 pp. Joyous comic lesbian novel. ISBN 1-56280-108-2 9.95

OPEN HOUSE by Pat Welch. 176 pp. 4th Helen Black Mystery. ISBN 1-56280-102-3 10.95

ONCE MORE WITH FEELING by Peggy J. Herring. 240 pp. Lighthearted, loving romantic adventure. ISBN 1-56280-089-2 10.95

FOREVER by Evelyn Kennedy. 224 pp. Passionate romance — love overcoming all obstacles. ISBN 1-56280-094-9 10.95

WHISPERS by Kris Bruyer. 176 pp. Romantic ghost story ISBN 1-56280-082-5 10.95

NIGHT SONGS by Penny Mickelbury. 224 pp. 2nd Gianna Maglione Mystery. ISBN 1-56280-097-3 10.95

GETTING TO THE POINT by Teresa Stores. 256 pp. Classic southern Lesbian novel. ISBN 1-56280-100-7 10.95

PAINTED MOON by Karin Kallmaker. 224 pp. Delicious Kallmaker romance. ISBN 1-56280-075-2 10.95

THE MYSTERIOUS NAIAD edited by Katherine V. Forrest & Barbara Grier. 320 pp. Love stories by Naiad Press authors. ISBN 1-56280-074-4 14.95

DAUGHTERS OF A CORAL DAWN by Katherine V. Forrest. 240 pp. Tenth Anniversay Edition. ISBN 1-56280-104-X 10.95

BODY GUARD by Claire McNab. 208 pp. 6th Carol Ashton Mystery. ISBN 1-56280-073-6 10.95

CACTUS LOVE by Lee Lynch. 192 pp. Stories by the beloved storyteller. ISBN 1-56280-071-X 9.95

SECOND GUESS by Rose Beecham. 216 pp. 2nd Amanda Valentine Mystery. ISBN 1-56280-069-8 9.95

THE SURE THING by Melissa Hartman. 208 pp. L.A. earthquake romance. ISBN 1-56280-078-7 9.95

A RAGE OF MAIDENS by Lauren Wright Douglas. 240 pp. 6th Caitlin Reece Mystery. ISBN 1-56280-068-X 10.95

TRIPLE EXPOSURE by Jackie Calhoun. 224 pp. Romantic drama involving many characters. ISBN 1-56280-067-1 9.95

UP, UP AND AWAY by Catherine Ennis. 192 pp. Delightful romance. ISBN 1-56280-065-5 9.95

PERSONAL ADS by Robbi Sommers. 176 pp. Sizzling short stories. ISBN 1-56280-059-0 9.95

FLASHPOINT by Katherine V. Forrest. 256 pp. Lesbian blockbuster! ISBN 1-56280-043-4 22.95

CROSSWORDS by Penny Sumner. 256 pp. 2nd Victoria Cross Mystery. ISBN 1-56280-064-7 9.95

SWEET CHERRY WINE by Carol Schmidt. 224 pp. A novel of suspense. ISBN 1-56280-063-9 9.95

CERTAIN SMILES by Dorothy Tell. 160 pp. Erotic short stories. ISBN 1-56280-066-3 9.95

EDITED OUT by Lisa Haddock. 224 pp. 1st Carmen Ramirez Mystery. ISBN 1-56280-077-9 9.95

WEDNESDAY NIGHTS by Camarin Grae. 288 pp. Sexy adventure. ISBN 1-56280-060-4 10.95

SMOKEY O by Celia Cohen. 176 pp. Relationships on the playing field. ISBN 1-56280-057-4 9.95

KATHLEEN O'DONALD by Penny Hayes. 256 pp. Rose and Kathleen find each other and employment in 1909 NYC. ISBN 1-56280-070-1 9.95

STAYING HOME by Elisabeth Nonas. 256 pp. Molly and Alix want a baby . . . or do they? ISBN 1-56280-076-0 10.95

TRUE LOVE by Jennifer Fulton. 240 pp. Six lesbians searching for love in all the "right" places. ISBN 1-56280-035-3 10.95

GARDENIAS WHERE THERE ARE NONE by Molleen Zanger. 176 pp. Why is Melanie inextricably drawn to the old house? ISBN 1-56280-056-6 9.95

KEEPING SECRETS by Penny Mickelbury. 208 pp. 1st Gianna Maglione Mystery. ISBN 1-56280-052-3 9.95

THE ROMANTIC NAIAD edited by Katherine V. Forrest & Barbara Grier. 336 pp. Love stories by Naiad Press authors. ISBN 1-56280-054-X 14.95

UNDER MY SKIN by Jaye Maiman. 336 pp. 3rd Robin Miller Mystery. ISBN 1-56280-049-3. 10.95

STAY TOONED by Rhonda Dicksion. 144 pp. Cartoons — 1st collection since *Lesbian Survival Manual.* ISBN 1-56280-045-0 9.95

CAR POOL by Karin Kallmaker. 272pp. Lesbians on wheels and then some! ISBN 1-56280-048-5 10.95

NOT TELLING MOTHER: STORIES FROM A LIFE by Diane Salvatore. 176 pp. Her 3rd novel. ISBN 1-56280-044-2 9.95

GOBLIN MARKET by Lauren Wright Douglas. 240pp. 5th Caitlin Reece Mystery. ISBN 1-56280-047-7 10.95

LONG GOODBYES by Nikki Baker. 256 pp. 3rd Virginia Kelly Mystery. ISBN 1-56280-042-6 9.95

FRIENDS AND LOVERS by Jackie Calhoun. 224 pp. Mid-western Lesbian lives and loves. ISBN 1-56280-041-8 10.95

THE CAT CAME BACK by Hilary Mullins. 208 pp. Highly praised Lesbian novel. ISBN 1-56280-040-X 9.95

BEHIND CLOSED DOORS by Robbi Sommers. 192 pp. Hot, erotic short stories. ISBN 1-56280-039-6 9.95

CLAIRE OF THE MOON by Nicole Conn. 192 pp. See the movie — read the book! ISBN 1-56280-038-8 10.95

SILENT HEART by Claire McNab. 192 pp. Exotic Lesbian romance. ISBN 1-56280-036-1 10.95

HAPPY ENDINGS by Kate Brandt. 272 pp. Intimate conversations with Lesbian authors. ISBN 1-56280-050-7 10.95

THE SPY IN QUESTION by Amanda Kyle Williams. 256 pp. 4th Madison McGuire Mystery. ISBN 1-56280-037-X 9.95

SAVING GRACE by Jennifer Fulton. 240 pp. Adventure and romantic entanglement. ISBN 1-56280-051-5 9.95

THE YEAR SEVEN by Molleen Zanger. 208 pp. Women surviving in a new world. ISBN 1-56280-034-5 9.95

CURIOUS WINE by Katherine V. Forrest. 176 pp. Tenth Anniversary Edition. The most popular contemporary Lesbian love story. ISBN 1-56280-053-1 10.95

Audio Book (2 cassettes) ISBN 1-56280-105-8 16.95

CHAUTAUQUA by Catherine Ennis. 192 pp. Exciting, romantic adventure. ISBN 1-56280-032-9 9.95

A PROPER BURIAL by Pat Welch. 192 pp. 3rd Helen Black Mystery. ISBN 1-56280-033-7 9.95

SILVERLAKE HEAT: A Novel of Suspense by Carol Schmidt. 240 pp. Rhonda is as hot as Laney's dreams. ISBN 1-56280-031-0 9.95

LOVE, ZENA BETH by Diane Salvatore. 224 pp. The most talked about lesbian novel of the nineties! ISBN 1-56280-030-2 10.95

A DOORYARD FULL OF FLOWERS by Isabel Miller. 160 pp. Stories incl. 2 sequels to *Patience and Sarah.* ISBN 1-56280-029-9 9.95

MURDER BY TRADITION by Katherine V. Forrest. 288 pp. 4th Kate Delafield Mystery.	ISBN 1-56280-002-7	10.95
THE EROTIC NAIAD edited by Katherine V. Forrest & Barbara Grier. 224 pp. Love stories by Naiad Press authors.	ISBN 1-56280-026-4	13.95
DEAD CERTAIN by Claire McNab. 224 pp. 5th Carol Ashton Mystery.	ISBN 1-56280-027-2	9.95
CRAZY FOR LOVING by Jaye Maiman. 320 pp. 2nd Robin Miller Mystery.	ISBN 1-56280-025-6	9.95
STONEHURST by Barbara Johnson. 176 pp. Passionate regency romance.	ISBN 1-56280-024-8	10.95
INTRODUCING AMANDA VALENTINE by Rose Beecham. 256 pp. 1st Amanda Valentine Mystery.	ISBN 1-56280-021-3	9.95
UNCERTAIN COMPANIONS by Robbi Sommers. 204 pp. Steamy, erotic novel.	ISBN 1-56280-017-5	9.95
A TIGER'S HEART by Lauren W. Douglas. 240 pp. 4th Caitlin Reece Mystery.	ISBN 1-56280-018-3	9.95
PAPERBACK ROMANCE by Karin Kallmaker. 256 pp. A delicious romance.	ISBN 1-56280-019-1	9.95
MORTON RIVER VALLEY by Lee Lynch. 304 pp. Lee Lynch at her best!	ISBN 1-56280-016-7	9.95
THE LAVENDER HOUSE MURDER by Nikki Baker. 224 pp. 2nd Virginia Kelly Mystery.	ISBN 1-56280-012-4	9.95
PASSION BAY by Jennifer Fulton. 224 pp. Passionate romance, virgin beaches, tropical skies.	ISBN 1-56280-028-0	10.95
STICKS AND STONES by Jackie Calhoun. 208 pp. Contemporary lesbian lives and loves.	ISBN 1-56280-020-5	9.95
Audio Book (2 cassettes)	ISBN 1-56280-106-6	16.95
DELIA IRONFOOT by Jeane Harris. 192 pp. Adventure for Delia and Beth in the Utah mountains.	ISBN 1-56280-014-0	9.95
UNDER THE SOUTHERN CROSS by Claire McNab. 192 pp. Romantic nights Down Under.	ISBN 1-56280-011-6	9.95
GRASSY FLATS by Penny Hayes. 256 pp. Lesbian romance in the '30s.	ISBN 1-56280-010-8	9.95
A SINGULAR SPY by Amanda K. Williams. 192 pp. 3rd Madison McGuire Mystery.	ISBN 1-56280-008-6	8.95
THE END OF APRIL by Penny Sumner. 240 pp. 1st Victoria Cross Mystery.	ISBN 1-56280-007-8	8.95
HOUSTON TOWN by Deborah Powell. 208 pp. A Hollis Carpenter Mystery.	ISBN 1-56280-006-X	8.95
KISS AND TELL by Robbi Sommers. 192 pp. Scorching stories by the author of *Pleasures.*	ISBN 1-56280-005-1	10.95

STILL WATERS by Pat Welch. 208 pp. 2nd Helen Black Mystery.
ISBN 0-941483-97-5 9.95

TO LOVE AGAIN by Evelyn Kennedy. 208 pp. Wildly romantic love story. ISBN 0-941483-85-1 9.95

IN THE GAME by Nikki Baker. 192 pp. 1st Virginia Kelly Mystery. ISBN 1-56280-004-3 9.95

AVALON by Mary Jane Jones. 256 pp. A Lesbian Arthurian romance. ISBN 0-941483-96-7 9.95

STRANDED by Camarin Grae. 320 pp. Entertaining, riveting adventure. ISBN 0-941483-99-1 9.95

THE DAUGHTERS OF ARTEMIS by Lauren Wright Douglas. 240 pp. 3rd Caitlin Reece Mystery. ISBN 0-941483-95-9 9.95

CLEARWATER by Catherine Ennis. 176 pp. Romantic secrets of a small Louisiana town. ISBN 0-941483-65-7 8.95

THE HALLELUJAH MURDERS by Dorothy Tell. 176 pp. 2nd Poppy Dillworth Mystery. ISBN 0-941483-88-6 8.95

SECOND CHANCE by Jackie Calhoun. 256 pp. Contemporary Lesbian lives and loves. ISBN 0-941483-93-2 9.95

BENEDICTION by Diane Salvatore. 272 pp. Striking, contemporary romantic novel. ISBN 0-941483-90-8 9.95

BLACK IRIS by Jeane Harris. 192 pp. Caroline's hidden past . . .
ISBN 0-941483-68-1 8.95

TOUCHWOOD by Karin Kallmaker. 240 pp. Loving, May/ December romance. ISBN 0-941483-76-2 9.95

COP OUT by Claire McNab. 208 pp. 4th Carol Ashton Mystery.
ISBN 0-941483-84-3 9.95

THE BEVERLY MALIBU by Katherine V. Forrest. 288 pp. 3rd Kate Delafield Mystery. ISBN 0-941483-48-7 10.95

THAT OLD STUDEBAKER by Lee Lynch. 272 pp. Andy's affair with Regina and her attachment to her beloved car.
ISBN 0-941483-82-7 9.95

PASSION'S LEGACY by Lori Paige. 224 pp. Sarah is swept into the arms of Augusta Pym in this delightful historical romance.
ISBN 0-941483-81-9 8.95

THE PROVIDENCE FILE by Amanda Kyle Williams. 256 pp. 2nd Madison McGuire Mystery. ISBN 0-941483-92-4 8.95

I LEFT MY HEART by Jaye Maiman. 320 pp. 1st Robin Miller Mystery. ISBN 0-941483-72-X 10.95

THE PRICE OF SALT by Patricia Highsmith (writing as Claire Morgan). 288 pp. Classic lesbian novel, first issued in 1952 . . . acknowledged by its author under her own, very famous, name.
ISBN 1-56280-003-5 9.95

SIDE BY SIDE by Isabel Miller. 256 pp. From beloved author of *Patience and Sarah.* ISBN 0-941483-77-0 9.95

STAYING POWER: LONG TERM LESBIAN COUPLES by Susan E. Johnson. 352 pp. Joys of coupledom. ISBN 0-941-483-75-4 14.95

SLICK by Camarin Grae. 304 pp. Exotic, erotic adventure. ISBN 0-941483-74-6 9.95

NINTH LIFE by Lauren Wright Douglas. 256 pp. 2nd Caitlin Reece Mystery. ISBN 0-941483-50-9 8.95

PLAYERS by Robbi Sommers. 192 pp. Sizzling, erotic novel. ISBN 0-941483-73-8 9.95

MURDER AT RED ROOK RANCH by Dorothy Tell. 224 pp. 1st Poppy Dillworth Mystery. ISBN 0-941483-80-0 8.95

LESBIAN SURVIVAL MANUAL by Rhonda Dicksion. 112 pp. Cartoons! ISBN 0-941483-71-1 8.95

A ROOM FULL OF WOMEN by Elisabeth Nonas. 256 pp. Contemporary Lesbian lives. ISBN 0-941483-69-X 9.95

THEME FOR DIVERSE INSTRUMENTS by Jane Rule. 208 pp. Powerful romantic lesbian stories. ISBN 0-941483-63-0 8.95

CLUB 12 by Amanda Kyle Williams. 288 pp. Espionage thriller featuring a lesbian agent! ISBN 0-941483-64-9 8.95

DEATH DOWN UNDER by Claire McNab. 240 pp. 3rd Carol Ashton Mystery. ISBN 0-941483-39-8 9.95

MONTANA FEATHERS by Penny Hayes. 256 pp. Vivian and Elizabeth find love in frontier Montana. ISBN 0-941483-61-4 8.95

LIFESTYLES by Jackie Calhoun. 224 pp. Contemporary Lesbian lives and loves. ISBN 0-941483-57-6 9.95

WILDERNESS TREK by Dorothy Tell. 192 pp. Six women on vacation learning "new" skills. ISBN 0-941483-60-6 8.95

MURDER BY THE BOOK by Pat Welch. 256 pp. 1st Helen Black Mystery. ISBN 0-941483-59-2 9.95

THERE'S SOMETHING I'VE BEEN MEANING TO TELL YOU Ed. by Loralee MacPike. 288 pp. Gay men and lesbians coming out to their children. ISBN 0-941483-44-4 9.95

LIFTING BELLY by Gertrude Stein. Ed. by Rebecca Mark. 104 pp. Erotic poetry. ISBN 0-941483-51-7 10.95

AFTER THE FIRE by Jane Rule. 256 pp. Warm, human novel by this incomparable author. ISBN 0-941483-45-2 8.95

THREE WOMEN by March Hastings. 232 pp. Golden oldie. A triangle among wealthy sophisticates. ISBN 0-941483-43-6 8.95

PLEASURES by Robbi Sommers. 204 pp. Unprecedented eroticism. ISBN 0-941483-49-5 8.95

EDGEWISE by Camarin Grae. 372 pp. Spellbinding adventure. ISBN 0-941483-19-3 9.95

FATAL REUNION by Claire McNab. 224 pp. 2nd Carol Ashton Mystery. ISBN 0-941483-40-1 10.95

IN EVERY PORT by Karin Kallmaker. 228 pp. Jessica's sexy, adventuresome travels. ISBN 0-941483-37-7 9.95

OF LOVE AND GLORY by Evelyn Kennedy. 192 pp. Exciting WWII romance. ISBN 0-941483-32-0 10.95

CLICKING STONES by Nancy Tyler Glenn. 288 pp. Love transcending time. ISBN 0-941483-31-2 9.95

SOUTH OF THE LINE by Catherine Ennis. 216 pp. Civil War adventure. ISBN 0-941483-29-0 8.95

WOMAN PLUS WOMAN by Dolores Klaich. 300 pp. Supurb Lesbian overview. ISBN 0-941483-28-2 9.95

THE FINER GRAIN by Denise Ohio. 216 pp. Brilliant young college lesbian novel. ISBN 0-941483-11-8 8.95

OCTOBER OBSESSION by Meredith More. Josie's rich, secret Lesbian life. ISBN 0-941483-18-5 8.95

BEFORE STONEWALL: THE MAKING OF A GAY AND LESBIAN COMMUNITY by Andrea Weiss & Greta Schiller. 96 pp., 25 illus. ISBN 0-941483-20-7 7.95

OSTEN'S BAY by Zenobia N. Vole. 204 pp. Sizzling adventure romance set on Bonaire. ISBN 0-941483-15-0 8.95

LESSONS IN MURDER by Claire McNab. 216 pp. 1st Carol Ashton Mystery. ISBN 0-941483-14-2 9.95

YELLOWTHROAT by Penny Hayes. 240 pp. Margarita, bandit, kidnaps Julia. ISBN 0-941483-10-X 8.95

SAPPHISTRY: THE BOOK OF LESBIAN SEXUALITY by Pat Califia. 3d edition, revised. 208 pp. ISBN 0-941483-24-X 10.95

CHERISHED LOVE by Evelyn Kennedy. 192 pp. Erotic Lesbian love story. ISBN 0-941483-08-8 10.95

THE SECRET IN THE BIRD by Camarin Grae. 312 pp. Striking, psychological suspense novel. ISBN 0-941483-05-3 8.95

TO THE LIGHTNING by Catherine Ennis. 208 pp. Romantic Lesbian 'Robinson Crusoe' adventure. ISBN 0-941483-06-1 8.95

DREAMS AND SWORDS by Katherine V. Forrest. 192 pp. Romantic, erotic, imaginative stories. ISBN 0-941483-03-7 8.95

MEMORY BOARD by Jane Rule. 336 pp. Memorable novel about an aging Lesbian couple. ISBN 0-941483-02-9 10.95

THE ALWAYS ANONYMOUS BEAST by Lauren Wright Douglas. 224 pp. 1st Caitlin Reece Mystery. ISBN 0-941483-04-5 8.95